NAKED ME

by

CHRISTIAN WINN

DOCK STREET PRESS

SEATTLE

www.dockstreetpress.com

These stories first appeared: "One Thing To Take," in *Revolver*; "The Dirtiest Hamburger in the
World," in *Gulf Coast*; "Naked Me," in *The Chicago Tribune's Printers Row Journal*; "Rough Cut," in
McSweeney's; "Where He's Living Now," in *Hayden's Ferry Review*; "North," in *Handful of Dust*;
"Dentists," in *Chattahoochee Review*; "All Her Famous Dead," in *The Chicago Tribune's Printers Row
Journal*; "Mr. Formal," in *Greensboro Review*; "Proof," in *Every Day Fiction*;
"False History," in *Bat City Review*.

www.dockstreetpress.com

ISBN: 978-0-9910657-2-1

Printed in the U.S.A.

For my friends, my friends.

CONTENTS

NAKED ME

ONE THING TO TAKE

It was a drink-on-the-job job. Gordo's. My Uncle C's hamburger stand down on Shilshole Bay. Summer 1989. Everything smelling like Coppertone and grease. Everything retreating across the wide bell of sky.

This was a few months after Mom and I moved in with Uncle C, the year after Dad left. Billy was the one who'd come by Gordo's afternoons with bourbon and lemonade. It was the summer I turned nineteen, and Billy was my older sister's boyfriend. Or, I guess he was both our boyfriends. He'd see her up at Western on weekends, and me the rest of the time.

Billy was handsome in a gangly way—long and sharp, sweet despite what he did with my sister and me. And really it was us who let him do it. Uncle C was handsome, too, but he was a creep, even if he did pay me okay and drink with Billy and me while I sold peanut butter milkshakes and double Fat-Boys to housewives and marina dads and kids I'd gone to school with.

When Billy'd come around and hand off tall cups, Uncle C would sit on the reach-in and look at him like nice work fucking both my nieces. Then he'd look me up and down, nodding.

After Dad, Mom had pretty well lost herself, and maybe so had I. Uncle C, she said, was just trying to help us, in his own way. Mostly by letting Mom sleep in his bed. Mostly by saying sorry about his piece of shit little brother. Mostly by cornering Billy and getting stories off him. Mom came around some days. Sat out front in the sun, wearing cutoffs and her red bikini top. Billy'd give her a nice tall drink. Uncle C would sit beside her and she'd lift her feet onto his lap where he'd rub her arches. This always made her smile, which was one thing to take from all that time.

THE DIRTIEST HAMBURGER
IN THE WORLD

It was the first week of July when Drew came over at 9am, told me his mother was hunched in her bedroom closet pretending she was a rabbit. He said she was eating a Pop-Tart with tiny buck-toothed bites. He wanted it to be funny, but I know he was scared. We were fourteen. It was 1980, and six months earlier Drew Har-well's family—he, his father, his mother—had moved next door to my father and me on Sonora Avenue, a street that cut a line between the good and bad neighborhoods of the mid-sized Cali-fornia town where I'd lived my whole life. Two blocks north the houses with swimming pools and three-car garages started up. Two blocks south there were yellow, un-mowed lawns and bars on first-floor windows.

We lived in what Drew's father called the DMZ—"The De-Mexicanized Zone," he'd say in his deep, round voice, tilting his head sideways like the young Marlon Brando—but my father told me we didn't call it that. Both our houses were nice enough—three bedrooms, two bathrooms, front porches, built by the same crew in the 1940's—and Drew had become my best friend. He was quiet, spoke softly, and always had smart, if small, things to say. He was good-looking, tall and thin, tanned and blond, so unlike me who was short, somewhat pale and wide. His mother was beautiful, golden blonde and long-legged, and lately she'd been going a little crazy. She'd taken to hiding in the basement, or in closets. My mother, she was living in Seattle with an airline pilot she met in 1977 at her tennis club. His name was Clark, and my father and I hated him. My father and I have always wished for things the world won't give up, and those years we quietly wished my mother would come back, but that didn't ever happen. I felt bad for Drew, losing his mom slowly, but I thought he was luckier than me to at least still have her around, even if that morning he had to tell me she was hopping around saying, "Gimmie some carrots or it's down the rabbit hole I go."

When Drew came over I was supposed to be cleaning up the cans and cigarette butts in our backyard and sweeping the back patio. He slipped through the gate that joined our yards.

"You gotta check this out," he said. "My mom has completely lost it."

He cautiously waved me toward him, and we tiptoed across the lawn, through their back door, and into his parent's bedroom where I saw his mother glance up at me with a skewed recognition, saying, "Bradley Owens, do you want to hop, hop around with me? It's super fun!" She looked absolutely sincere, and graceful, and I thought that it would be easy to fall in love with something like her.

8

She looked like Grace Kelly with a sweet down-turned mouth, but her eyes, they missed things.

I looked at Drew, told her, "No thank you." The room was dim and smelled like baby powder; a Glen Campbell song rose loudly from the hi-fi.

He shrugged and winked, still trying to play it off as nothing, and we walked back outside, his beautiful mother saying, "Bounce-bounce my boys! Bye-bye!"

"I told you," Drew said. "She's gonzo."

A silent, awkward moment passed, Drew smiling and nodding, looking up into the big maple tree that canopied the driveway.

"Freaky," I said, but felt stupid for saying it.

"Yep."

"Should we call your dad?"

"No."

Drew said he wanted to walk downtown to where his father managed the Ace Hardware store, tell him face to face, see what he thought. He figured his dad might buy us lunch or give him grocery money, and we could use the cash for baseball cards, Slurpees, whatever. Then another strange thing happened.

"Oh, boys!" we heard, and Mrs. Harwell came hopping toward us from the side yard. My face flashed hot, and my earlobes burned as they always have in impossible, embarrassing moments. Drew laughed again in a short, nervous burst, his eyes widening.

"Don't you remember, Drewsy," she said, so happy as she hopped toward us, "how it was up in Oregon? We'd go to Cannon Beach, that one house . . . you were so little then. We'd dig in the sand, and play rabbits, singing *Here comes Peter Cottontail, hopping down the . . ."*

"Mom."

"*. . . bunny trail.*"

"Stop, Mother!"

She did stop, ten strides from us, and hopped in place. Drew's wide eyes narrowed, and he held them on her. I looked away toward my backyard, wondering just how a grown woman could be lost, so childlike. It didn't seem wholly like a wrong thing, but I knew how I'd feel if I were Drew.

"Mom," Drew said. "Go back inside."

"I'm ready to go see your father with you."

"He'll be home later. Bradley and me are going to get that stuff for you."

"Bradley and I," she said.

"Let's get you back inside, Mom," Drew said.

"I'll be right back," I said, stepping slowly away. "Just need to get some money."

"Wait, Bradley," Drew said. "Please."

He went to his mother's side, took her arm, and led her back in, whispering unknowable things to her, making her laugh a little, calming her. In a moment he was back, and we went over to my house where I quickly finished cleaning up, put on some shoes and a ball cap, grabbed the ten dollars my father had left for me.

"She'll be okay?"

"Sure," Drew said. "Let's go."

—

It had been a cooler summer, but that morning the heat was gathering early. Before Drew came over, I'd been sorting baseball cards on the backyard picnic table, organizing them by team, setting the doubles aside to trade with Rusty or his brother Alan, our friends up the block. My father was at his office in San Francisco where he copy-edited textbooks. He was there a lot those days. He biked to the train station and took the weekday 7:27 express into the city, and sometimes he didn't get home until eight or nine, stopping at The Poppy Seed, a bar two blocks from the train station. He'd have a bourbon, a few beers, ride home with his tie folded into the pocket of his suit, and if I was around he'd ask me, depending on the season, how my baseball or basketball or soccer was going.

"Fine, Pops," I'd say, though a week before that morning Drew came to me, I'd quit my summer league baseball team and not told my father. I'd quit because the coach, Mr. Delaney, pushed me to the ground one day at practice as Drew and I were playing at being Tom Seaver and Johnny Bench, bantering our memorized play-by-play routine. Mr. Delaney got angry.

"You're a nothing little screw-off, Owens," he said, pointing down and standing over me in a hard, cruel manner.

I walked off the field, walked the two miles home in my catcher's gear. Drew met me half an hour later, said that he'd quit too, and that was something for Drew. He was the best player in our league. He was six-feet tall, left-handed, and already threw an eighty-five-mile-an-hour fastball. The coach must have called twenty times pleading him to return, saying he was sorry, saying that I'd had it coming, that I was holding back Drew and the team. Drew said no, that I was his friend, that it was both of us, or neither. When Mr. Delaney said fine, I could come back to the team then, Drew said no again, a proud moment in my life. Through the ordeal Drew's father backed him up too, admiring his loyalty and gall. "My boy's got balls," he'd tell us. "More than Delaney." And that summer Drew and I practiced ourselves, waited for high school tryouts in the fall.

That summer my dad and I would sit with Drew and his father at night, either in our backyard or theirs, while Drew's mother read her books or watched television. In the backyard, the four of us draped ourselves on lawn furniture, the dads drinking cans of Lucky Lager, Drew and I bottles of Dr. Pepper. The dads told stories, and we mostly listened. Drew and I learned a lot about women's breasts and drinking and fist fights, a lot about the hopeful ways of men. Drew's father had enlisted in the Navy after high school, had done four tours during the war, but he never talked about the fighting. The way he told it the war sounded like fun, but we couldn't really know. We just loved to hear his stories about foreign ports with lusty Vietnamese women waiting, breath baited, skirts short. My dad told about college days, drinking and hazing and pranking. He talked about San Francisco protests, naked dancing in Golden Gate Park.

I understand now that Drew's father and mine were very different people, and the fact we all laughed hard that summer— even if we didn't know precisely at what—is something rare.

Perhaps our fathers stayed strong this way so that the women they were losing could become secondary, so that the good stories about drinking and desire and laughter could stand tall and remain important.

Downtown was two and a half miles if we walked part way along the cemented aqueduct creek that cut behind our neighborhood and ran out to the bay. We often rode our Schwinns, but walked around town more after we quit baseball. We had time to kill, and downtown was a good trek for us because there were places to stop along the way, hidden folds of our city for Drew and I to discover new and revelatory things.

The summer of 1980 we seemed to find so much. We found a switchblade knife and a little baggie of marijuana wedged into a storm drain on Middlefield Street. I was afraid to smoke the dope, but kept the knife, and we traded the pot to a kid named Derrick Jackson who lived up our street for half a brick of firecrackers. We found a passed-out drunk woman, hair matted and filthy, beside a dumpster in the alley running behind the Main Street shops. We found a box of old Playboys on the bank of the creek, and after studying them closely—the muted soft skin, the mysterious turns of hip and chest—we sold them for a dollar apiece to kids hanging out at Mitchell Park.

That summer we also discovered a ten-foot plastic hamburger that sat in a wide parking lot under two eucalyptus trees between Ling's Chinese Restaurant and the Tip Top Tavern four blocks south of Main Street. We loved the hamburger. We had no idea just what it was doing there, but it always made us laugh—its giant yellow bun, its sesame seeds, the charred black hue of the patty, the unreal bright green of the lettuce—just sitting there dusty and covered with leaves. It lay next to the brick wall of Ling's, and Drew and I would climb up on it, check out our Playboys, or talk, or recite new jokes we had heard. Drew sometimes stole cigarettes from his father, and sitting on the hamburger was where we smoked them.

"Hungry?" Drew asked me that morning as we strode up our block, kicking pebbles.

We walked up Sonora and onto Middlefield, feeling the late morning heat. I was only five foot two, not getting my growth spurt until I was eighteen, and Drew walked in long, graceful strides. I had to high-step it to keep up.

"What about your mother?" I asked Drew, imagining her reading or talking to herself in that dim fragrant bedroom. Drew was silent, stoic. We hopped the barrier fence, began walking the bank. The gray cement of the creek was almost dry. A three-foot-wide trickling band of green water lay across the twenty-foot bed.

"I don't know," Drew said. "You saw enough to know. What about your mother, Bradley?"

I knew he hated what was happening, but this made me mad. "You've never met her," I said. "And you probably never will."

"She never hops around?"

Drew had said nothing about the strange actions of his mother prior to that morning, and he'd never let me in to see her. I felt he was sorry for being casual about it earlier, wishing he hadn't showed her off like a joke. And I was sorry we were almost arguing, something we never did. Drew looked down at the dry weeds and pale dirt, shook his head, scuffed his feet.

"Sorry." He held his head low.

"It's cool, Drew," I said. "Really." I patted him on the shoulder, and he patted me back. "It's fine."

I had vaguely learned of his mother's oddity from his father who some nights drinking beers on the back porch said things like, "The woman has started hooting like an owl," or "She's taken to playing monkey games in bed." My dad would laugh a little nervously, or a little pleasurably, depending on how much he'd drunk. Drew would look at the grass, chew his nails, crook his neck skyward. I was sorry then, that morning, to have ever made fun of his gorgeous mother, and felt some new level of knowledge—empathy, or sorrow, or self-loathing—rise up into me.

"Do you want to go to the hamburger now?" I asked him.

"Yeah. Well, not yet."

"Downtown first?"

"Let's go see my dad," Drew said, bending down to pick up a playing card that was lying by itself on the bank. It was the jack of clubs, and he held it between the middle and index fingers of his left hand, dusted it with his right thumb.

"Think I can toss it across?"

We stopped and Drew cocked his wrist, flicked the card out over the creek bed where it dipped, spun tightly then rose, climbing and hanging. We watched it stop, weightless, then fall, fluttering to land in a patch of gray-green water where it floated, its corners curling upward.

"Smokes?"

"Fresh pack." He pulled out a box of Marlboro reds, waving them in the air.

We walked half a mile without saying anything while three younger kids we didn't know rode moto-cross bikes up and down the creek, shouting, hitting the brakes to skid the thick algae shallows. At Banner Street we hopped over the wall, and walked the mile to the hardware store. The streets were quieter than usual, and we talked about baseball and a girl named Francis Gove who had a crush on Drew. Francis was blonde and lithe and damned nice to look at. Francis was so pretty, looking something like I imagined Drew's mother had when she was sixteen, but Drew thought she was stuck up. Her family lived in a three-story house near the high school. They had a Mercedes and a Jaguar. Her father was a doctor. Drew had his father's distrust of the wealthy, even at fourteen.

That summer, my dad and I missed my mother more than ever. We were on the cusp of fully accepting that she wasn't coming back to us. We were in the last throws of hopefulness, and for my father that meant making too many sad, begging phone calls to Mom. He would phone her early in the morning, or after eleven at night, seemingly wanting to catch her at inconvenient or awkward times.

He spoke softly, almost cooing into the receiver, "We do miss you sweet cakes," or "The nicest *family* moved in next door," or even "Please, please, please woman, please woman." He called her all the time, but I don't think he knew that I'd sit in the next room and listen. Every once in a while, if he called after a few drinks, my father would cup his hand over the receiver's mouthpiece and make his voice sound like he was an airline pilot, trying to goad her about Clark. He would say: "Ladies and gentlemen this is your captain speaking—shhhhhkkk. We are currently cruising at 20,000 feet with a slight tailwind. The current temperature on the ground in San Francisco is 62 degrees, but fog is expected this evening— shhhhhkkk. And if you'll look out your window to the south you'll see a lonely son and father some 1,000 miles away—shhhhhkkk."

I was embarrassed for him—and still am—but happy that he was reaching out in his own odd way. He has never mentioned the phone calls, nor has my mother, and to remember them myself makes me wonder at the other cloaked moments of history my parents share only with each other.

At the Ace Hardware store Drew's father was helping a fat man in overalls pick out a circular saw. He saw us walk in and waved us his direction. The fat man had his wide back to us and he turned slowly, squinted at me, then Drew. He pointed and winked, nodding his round head. "This your boy?" he said.

"This one here is," Drew's father said, pulling his son close to him, Drew trying to muster a smile.

"Good looking kid," the fat man said. "Go ahead and wrap that saw up. I'll take it."

"Meet me in back, fellas," Mr. Harwell said, winking and grinning through a muted look of concern.

On the desk in Mr. Harwell's office was an ashtray, two neat stacks of paper, and a framed family portrait. The air was woven with smells of paint, fresh-cut wood, tacky rubber gaskets, and stale smoke. Above the desk was July's calendar picturing a nude woman cradling a chainsaw like a child. We both stared. I reached up and ran my fingers over her breasts, something one of us always did when we came to his dad's store. We loved those calendars—the pink and mysterious other side—but that day Drew just watched me, straight-faced.

"That's a nice set there, ain't it Bradley?" It was Mr. Harwell.

I snapped my hand back as he stepped in. "A nice set, sure, Mr. H.," I said.

"You boys finding any of that this summer?"

"Not yet, Mr. Harwell," I said.

"Well, keep looking," he said as he sat down at his desk. "And to what do I owe the pleasure this morning?"

I looked at my shoes as Drew started telling him the story about his mother. When Drew got to the word rabbit his Dad interrupted.

"Bradley," he said. "Would you mind giving us a moment?"

Drew looked at me and shrugged. I nodded and walked out into the store. A kid employee I hadn't seen before was securing a paint bucket in the motorized mixing machine, and I watched him set it up, switch it on. The machine whirred, hummed, vibrated the bucket so quickly it blurred like the wings of a dragonfly. I stood with my hands in my pockets waiting, wondering how Drew was piecing together the events of this morning. Transfixed, I watched the mixer, oddly comforted, somehow equating this new motion with the solemn words being passed between a father and son in the back room.

—

When I talked to my mother on the phone—every other week, or so—I found myself getting angry with her, and started half-way making up violent little stories intended to scare her, maybe make her feel like she needed to be around for me. It started with me telling her I'd punched my baseball coach in the gut after he bitched Drew out for being lazy. My mother's reaction was to advise me to apologize, that I was way out of line, that I was almost a man now, and real men—men like Clark—don't punch other men, ever, especially their superiors.

I told her about stealing a switchblade knife from Joey Franklin, a kid at school. I told her that the girls down the block sunbathed topless in their front yard. I told her that a lady who moved in next door was practicing witchcraft. I told her that I hung out and smoked cigarettes on top of a ten-foot hamburger with a bunch of derelict kids who lived in foster homes. Then, once, later in the summer, and I am sorry for this still, I told her that I didn't think Dad loved me as much as she did, and that he had gotten drunk and slapped me around. "Bradley," she said. "You've just got to get a grip. Now, I know it's hard, but you've got to quit lying to me. I'm here, okay? And I'm staying here. Your father and I are *not* going to be together again."

I almost cried when she said it, so evenly, so matter-of-factly, but I thought of my father whispering sadly, maybe even weeping, into the phone. I did not want to be that man, and I held off. After that I quit with those stories.

—

Drew found me sifting through bins of screws and nails, admiring the uncountable mass of them, wondering who made all these gray little spikes.

He walked to me quickly. "Let's get."

"How many do you think are in there?" I pointed to the screw barrel.

"Dad gave me twenty-five dollars," Drew said. "He wants us to pick up her prescription."

We walked out of the hardware store toward Bergmand's Pharmacy. It was a block away, around the corner on Main where the street crowded with men and women on their lunch break.

That day in Bergmand's Pharmacy I stole packs of cards and Drew picked up a small-framed photograph of Amelia Earhart, asking me, "Do you think my mom would like this?"

"It seems nice."

Drew tucked it into the waistband of his pants, and we walked to the prescriptions counter where Drew talked to Bergmand in a hushed voice.

"Your father just called," Bergmand said. "It'll be twenty-two dollars."

"I only have twenty," Drew lied.

"You'll have to bring the rest in later," Bergmand said, leaning over the counter, giving us the hard stare. "This afternoon."

"My dad," Drew asked. "Can he bring it in tomorrow?"

"Come on, Drew."

"Shit, it's for my mother, Mr. B."

"Watch that mouth," Bergmand said. "I know who it's for." He crossed his arms, shook his long, pointy head, agreeing to take the twenty.

"Make certain she reads the label, gets the dosage right."

"I know how this goes."

"Listen, son. It's important."

"I *know* that," Drew said, and we both stared Bergmand down. He held Drew's eyes for a long moment, snapping the twenty from between his fingers, then coolly looking toward the front door as two older ladies walked in yakking away.

A minute later Drew and I stepped into the heated midday, Drew slipping the cylinder of pills into his jeans pocket. "He's such an asshole," I said.

"Got the cards?"

"Seven packs."

"Fuck-face Bergmand," Drew said, and we took off running.

I had been to visit my mother three times since she moved north, and had gone once earlier that summer. She never came to us, and she never, in those early years of separation, allowed my father to come to that clean, ranch-style house where she and Clark lived in Seattle's Magnolia neighborhood. Clark was always kind enough to me, but he was calculating, sterile, and he never seemed like a man with heart, with passion. He and my mother didn't laugh often, though it was clear they were pleased enough with each other. Visiting them made me anxious. In Seattle, Mother would take me to Boeing's flight museum, to the top of the Space Needle, to the

Science Center, and the Pike Place Market, wanting me to love the city, but more importantly, the man she had chosen over my father and me. But, I couldn't, and I knew I never would.

Down Main I ran after Drew, holding the packs of cards tight to my waist as he took a right and headed for Ling's and the hamburger. I caught him down the block where the air got quieter, more desolate, the houses smaller and shorter. A red Chevy Impala rolled slowly by us, the high school kids inside yelling, "Bang! Motherfuckers! Bang!" They pointed a finger like a gun toward us. Drew immediately flipped them off, so uncharacteristic for him, and this scared me, made me think those kids would turn around, mess with us. Drew didn't seem scared, so we just kept walking, and they kept driving.

The sight of the hamburger was always shocking and odd and funny. It was fantastically satisfying, approaching that big colorful plastic mound from the parking lot. Sitting there beneath those trees, at the edge of that parking lot, it looked to me beautifully ludicrous and exaggerated. Drew and I walked to the burger, propped ourselves up on it. I handed him three packs of baseball cards, and we began peeling back the waxed paper, smelling and chomping the bright pink gum.

"You know what I think of doing sometimes?" Drew said, thumbing through his first pack.

"Getting us killed by flipping off those big dudes in the Impala?"

"Those assholes."

"Big fuckers."

"Besides that," Drew said, flashing a Johnny Bench card in front of my face. "I think about crawling into this burger, some-how pulling the top bun off, crawling inside. I want to live in here." He punched the burger and a low, precise rumble moved through us and into the air.

"I've dreamt about it," he continued. "You and me, we could set up a really cool room, have parties, invite girls over."

"Francis Gove," I said. "And her friend with the big jugs, Colleen."

"My mom wouldn't be around doing all that goofy shit."

"She's okay."

"You think?" Drew said, reaching into his back pocket, un-folding a yellow slip of stationary paper. He was shaking. "Listen to this: *My dearest Drew, Today the colored hills are a frog burning green, the common sky is a tortured red pond. If you might crumble bones, I might bake with them, I might form them into a new broken being. I wish you could know me, and one day you will. I made you, son. You should know, your father whispers this in his sleep: 'God is only a pile of feathers in a windless room.'*"

"Holy shit," I said.

"She gave this to me yesterday. What the hell, Bradley?" His voice quavered.

"Maybe she just wanted you to have something," I said, look-ing across the dry, oil-spotted parking lot, smelling eucalyptus leaves mingling with the acrid, yeasty garbage from the Tip Top Tavern. "I wish my mom wrote me notes."

"Don't lie."

"She just lectures me from 1,500 miles away."

Drew ran a finger over the dusty hamburger, drawing a cartoon face without a mouth. I opened another pack of cards.

"No mothers here," Drew finally said, smiling, tucking the note back in his pocket. "We live in the burger, we don't think about them."

We sat on the hamburger then and smoked, and mixed with the afternoon heat it made me a little nauseous.

"Look at that piece of shit," Drew said, as an old green pickup with gray bondo patches above the wheel-wells and on the hood drove into the empty lot. Doug Clayton was driving, a kid two years older who lived down off Middlefield, someone we knew but never liked. Two kids sat in the back, one with a Led Zeppelin t-shirt on, the other one heavy-set and shirtless, red freckles dotting his shoulders.

"I can't believe he got that thing running," I said.

"He's a loser duct tape mechanic," Drew said. "That's what Dad would call him."

Clayton parked beside the hamburger, and lumbered his awkward body out of the still-running truck. "You toads have a cigarette or three?" he said, showing the wide gap between his front teeth that always made him look friendlier than he truly was. He was a big, ambling kid, and his size made him think he was tough.

"You have any cash?" I said, jumping down, trying to seem mean.

"Give me a break, Owens," he said, stepping toward me,

"Give me the cigarettes before I have to flex some muscle." He rolled the sleeves up on his t-shirt and flexed his biceps, stepping up to my face and laughing.

Drew slid off the hamburger. "Why's that so funny, Clayton?" he said. "Why do you think you're being funny?"

The other boys got out of the truck and came to stand behind Clayton as Drew stepped up to his face, pushing me aside. Clayton leaned back.

"I'm not in the mood for a laugh today," Drew said, looking as angry as I ever saw him, his voice tight. He pushed Clayton in the chest.

"Easy there, Harwell," Clayton said. "We just want a smoke."

"Yeah?" Drew said. "Here then." He reached into his jeans pocket, grabbed the cigarettes. As he did this, his mother's little yellow note fell from his pocket, slipping to the ground at the base of the hamburger. I quickly bent down, picked the paper up, crammed it into my own pocket without anyone noticing. I kept my hand on the note for a long moment, feeling a weight, a warmth reach through my fingers and forearm, my chest. Drew stared at the Marlboros, shook his head slowly, then he stepped back and heaved them at Clayton. The pack hollow-thudded against Clayton's chest and fell to his feet.

"What's up your ass?" the kid with the Zeppelin shirt said.

Clayton bent down. "Awfully generous of you, Harwell."

"Let's get out, Bradley." Drew shoved Clayton again, easier this time, and motioned for me to follow him, turning to walk away quickly.

"Your friend's a prick," Clayton said, flipping Drew off, doing a stupid hip-thrusting dance behind his back.

"You're the prick," I said, striding between the three of them, half expecting to get messed-up right there. I was ready, almost wanting to be hit and kicked, then to hit back and draw blood, inflict pain, show fully that I was on Drew's side of all things. But, they didn't even flinch, and I ran after Drew, leaving those three boys in the spotty shade beside the burger.

A week later the hamburger was gone. We returned to the lot with fresh cigarettes and more baseball cards, wanting to have a decent, peaceful time, and the big hamburger was gone, just a round smudge of dirt where it once stood. We were dumbstruck and angry. Our speculation was that Clayton and his friends loaded it into his fucked-up green truck and drove it off somewhere. We went looking for it at Clayton's house, but it wasn't there, and Clayton claimed he had no idea what the hell happened to it.

"Maybe someone ate the motherfucker," Clayton said, standing in his oily driveway, his dirty hands on those wide hips.

Later that fall, as the weather shifted toward jacket weather, the week after Drew's mother got back from her month in the hospital, the hamburger suddenly reappeared. Whoever had taken it dumped the burger into the dry creek, where it lay upside down, slightly cracked down the middle. Drew and I saw it on the way home from school, and we hooted and high-fived and climbed down into the creek. We turned the burger right-side up, and leaned against it, afraid we might break it if we sat on top. We thought of prying it open and finally climbing down inside, but somehow we couldn't desecrate it any further. We simply smoked our cigarettes right there, so happy to have gotten this one thing back, if for a short time.

Days later the first big rain came, and the creek filled up fast. Drew and I stood beneath umbrellas and watched from the Middlefield Bridge as the water rose and the burger began to lift and float downstream and away, the old grime and eucalyptus leaves washing into roiling water.

"We could be riding that thing," I said. "Steering it out into the bay."

"I wonder if we could?"

We saluted the burger as it slipped quickly through the murky water and under the Waverly Street Bridge, a block down.

After Drew shoved Clayton that summer afternoon he was anxious to get home. We cut along the creek, getting to our neighborhood near three. In front of his house I handed Drew back his mother's note.

"Oh shit," he said. "Don't tell anyone, okay? Not even our dads."

"You know I wouldn't."

"You wanna come in?"

"Okay."

His mother sat on the sofa wearing a satin robe and reading a paperback when we stepped into the living room. The curtains were drawn, and I couldn't imagine how she read in that shrouded light. She looked up slowly.

"Hello, boys." Her voice was friendly. "I'm reading Anne Rice. It's lovely. And a little scary. Listen." She began reading aloud as Drew walked over, crouched and whispered for her to come with him. They went into the bathroom, then into the bedroom, their muffled voices easing through the hallways to find me as I paced the living room, the dining room, the kitchen. I was oddly soothed in that space, and for a moment felt so tired, like I could fall to the floor and sleep for days. I shut my eyes and tried to feel the blood coursing through me, thinking about my own mother, and how she'd never met Drew, or the Harwells, how she never would, how she would never know about this day in my life. I wondered how my mother would have felt about Mrs. Harwell, her mild lunacy, and I thought that mostly, like me, it would make my mother sad.

Drew came out of the bedroom, and said, "She's gonna sleep for a while." He pulled the little picture of Amelia Earhart out of his trousers, and set it down on the kitchen counter.

"She'll like that," I said.

Mr. Harwell came home at four, and I left Drew with his mother and father, went home to watch television and oil my catcher's mitt, sort some more cards. At six Drew came over with his glove and a ball and we tossed it in the front yard, calling out plays and pitches, talking like Vin Scully and Harry Carey, hissing crowd noise through—as I remember them now—those perfect, honest moments. Dusk approached and my father rode up on his bike.

"Hey fellas," he said, and we said hey.

That night I watched the Oakland A's play the Detroit Tigers on television, the Monday night game, with Drew and my father. Drew and I ate spaghetti and drank soda; my father drank Lucky Lager. Though we expected Drew's father, he never came over. I wondered what he and Mrs. Harwell were doing next door, what words and actions passed between them. I pictured Mr. Harwell sitting next to her on the bed, reading that book aloud to her. I pictured him stroking her blonde hair, touching her cheek, telling her wise small things because this is what I would have done if I were him. I'm certain Drew wondered some of the same things, but we never asked each other the questions we shared that night. We acted as though nothing had shifted, but knew, as friends, that they had. We'd both seen how some things could begin to breakdown.

Sometime near ten, as the A's were closing out the Tigers, an aide car rolled up silently, its lights flashing, painting the neighborhood red and bright-blue as it parked in front of the Harwell's house.

"Shit," Drew said, standing, peeking through our picture window, then walking fast out the front door.

"Dear god," my father said, and we followed Drew as he ran to his own father.

Drew stood stiffly watching his father hug his mother tightly, as if his embrace could hold her together. His mother's face was pale, vacuous.

"It's a-okay, son," Drew's father said, as he lay her on the front lawn. "Just a reaction to some medication. A-okay."

The paramedics eased to his mother's side. She smiled as I came to Drew and we looked down at her perfect face. Drew mouthed, "Okay, Mom. A-okay."

My father patted Drew's father on the shoulder, and shook his head. Drew's father reached up in that moment, without looking, and he took my father's hand, squeezing it hard, weaving their fingers together tightly, earnestly, as they together gazed at Drew's mother.

"No big deal," one of the paramedics said. "Just gonna check her out at the hospital. Routine stuff."

They asked us to step aside, then lifted her onto a stretcher and loaded her into the aide car. Drew and his father hopped up into the rear compartment and knelt by her side as the driver shut the boxy rear doors and then just drove away. It all happened so quickly. The aide car was there, then it wasn't, and then my father and I were standing side by side on the Harwell's front lawn wondering what to say to each other.

A few other neighbors had emerged from their homes to stand and watch, but as the aide car drove off they slipped back inside.

"She is a beautiful woman," my father said. "That was hard to watch."

"Dad?" I said. "She'll be alright?"

"I think so, Bradley. Yes. A-Okay."

"They left their door open," I said, pointing.

"So they did," my father said, and I followed him up and onto the Harwell's porch where we could see television light skittering blue and silver across their living room walls.

We stepped inside. "Never have been in here," my dad said, almost tiptoeing over to their low brown sofa where he sat down, crossed his legs, and sniffed at the air. "Smells a little flowery."

"She likes her potpourri," I said, sitting next to him, "like Mom."

"That's true," he said, nodding his head slowly.

The post-game show was playing silently, and we sat there for a long time watching highlights and interviews. I tried to figure out what Bob Uecker was asking Tony Armas, but couldn't. It seemed oddly natural for us to be sitting in the Harwell's place, watching a mute television as their home creaked and settled with the cooling night. I felt we were keeping watch, making certain all this would still exist for our friends when they returned and tried to fit themselves back into this space.

My father put his arm around me. He was shaking a little. "Makes you wonder what next," he said, standing and turning off the television. "Like anything could happen to anybody."

"I guess it can," I said, following him through their front door and back home where in our living room I took his hand and told him goodnight.

NAKED ME

During the card games she'd come home to her apartment across the alley and undress. Her windows glowed with the white-gold light of five or six lamps and rows of fat candles. She always kept the curtains pegged open, showing the red carpet and the hardwoods and the soft blue paint of the kitchen and living room. And soon enough, she showed all of herself, too. Mostly she'd have boys along, but other times it was just her.

We'd be in the middle of a hand, Kenny the houseman running smack about how he was going to bust *all* of us tonight, or how he was going to buy another new car with his table-winnings this year, how he was going to send his kids to college on our bad play. I'd be reaching for a can of beer, or the gin, trying to figure how to get unstuck, how the fuck to win back the hundreds I'd lost that week, or the thousands I'd lost since I started sitting in the game two years prior. Her light would snap on, showing the dark velvet sofa, the Target-bought Matisse and Van Gogh prints, the bar top lined with green bottles. Then she'd emerge into the living room and unbutton herself, somebody at the table spotting her, then all of us getting up to stand on the dark balcony and watch the show. The dealer would keep an eye on our chip stacks while we crowded to the railing, lit cigarettes, and many of us murmured petty bullshit insults—"Come get the real goods, shorty," "You can't handle *this* truth ..." hip-thrusting, crotch grabbing, etc.

She was tall, and had tight red curls that fell to her pale, freckled shoulders when she pulled her blouse over her head and unhitched her bra and stood up against the window. Her building ran the length of the block across that pothole and garbage-rot alleyway. It was nerve-wracking and exhilarating when she went for her skirt, or jeans. Only sometimes did she wear panties, little pieces of lace that fell glowing to her floor. From our third-floor perch it was very *Rear Window,* and I mentioned this, and how Alfred Hitchcock himself was a dirty old fucker, but how he knew the power of inventing lives like the one in front of us.

"If he were around today," I said, watching her sit and sway, "we'd be in one of his films right now. I wish it were Grace Kelly over there, though."

They all looked at me like, what the fuck are you talking about now, Professor? That's what those players called me—The Professor—because those days, when I wasn't bartending I taught undergrad History at the university.

"Alfred Hitchcock? *The Birds*? *Psycho*?" I said. "How can you not know this?"

One of them stepped up, smiling with confidence, slapping my shoulder. "I loved Vince Vaughn in Psycho, Prof."

That moment describes this crowd of players perfectly—their confidence in untrue things—and why I wanted to win their money so badly, and why I was so frustrated because I couldn't.

I started explaining the plot of *Rear Window* because I wanted to prove I was something to that crowd, but at that moment the girl, who was alone that night, already lying across the living room carpet, V'd her legs and began to masturbate, and what could we do but watch in reverent and uncomfortable silence until Kenny the houseman came out and said show's over, let's get the game going, motherfuckers.

They all lingered a minute longer, but soon enough the game called them back. I stayed, though, leaning my elbows into the wooden railing, lighting another cigarette.

Afterward, she stood and walked naked into a back room. I cracked another beer and eyed the two other lighted apartments— a young couple held hands and watched television, laughing occasionally in the blue scatter-light; a middle-aged man sat at his dining room table drinking a bottle of wine, slowly slipping pieces into a jigsaw puzzle. The smoke and beer sped my heart and guts, getting me to thinking hard about money and my lack of it, about winning a monster pot or two, about getting at least back to even for the night, maybe for the week. I was in over $400 already that night, $300 of it on the books. But the night was young enough, it was maybe 1 am and the weekend game generally went through until daylight, sometimes all the way to noon. There always seemed to be time to get it back, but only rarely would it turn my way again once I started losing. I was a streaky player—going up, or going down, though down had more often been the case.

She returned to sit on her sofa wearing a yellow paisley robe that fell open across her hips. She read a little hardbound book and ran her fingers over her chest and belly. The book looked like dusty old poetry, or the bible. After a minute she set the book down between her legs and looked up directly at me on the shadowed balcony and smiled, titling her head, pulling her curls behind her ears. I stood straight and stepped back, embarrassed and aroused. Then she stood and walked to her glass door. She pulled her hair up, let it fall, swaying and posing for herself reflected in the glass, it seemed.

She walked back toward the kitchen, and I heard the clatter of chips behind me, someone yelling about the run of the cards and I remembered what I was there for, returned to the game, some kid in a Steelers jersey who I didn't even know, saying, "Jesus, Professor, you rubbing one out out there, or what?" then knuckle-bumping the guy next to him.

I shook my head, said, "Something like that," and sat down to count the chips I had left.

It was a floating, illegal card game—backroom and cash-only and moving from suburban garage to cheap Garden City rental to warehouse out near the airport so as to avoid trouble with cops and neighbors—run by a few guys who'd moved in from Montana, and who took a substantial rake, and who had evidently been living for ten years off the money the game generated. We played with intricately patterned, brightly-colored old clay chips that had come out of a Montana roadhouse. NO CASH VALUE was scripted across each chip, in case of a bust. Who knew if those words would create an out, a loophole? As far as I knew, the game had never been busted, even though the stakes were pretty high for a little city like ours. The most I ever saw on the table at one time was probably $25,000, though my buy-ins rarely exceeded $1,000, which was at the top-side of what I ever had in my bank account.

That summer the game had landed in a sandstone apartment downtown, close to the bars I frequented and walking distance of my apartment, a circumstance and temptation I often couldn't avoid, or didn't want to, at that point in my life.

I was 31, and had finished my master's coursework in History a year earlier. I was supposed to be working on my thesis and applying for jobs, though all that was in a lull. Cards and work and walking our little city in between everything and wondering what next? what now? had come to fill my time. Most of my close friends from graduate school had moved, starting Ph.Ds or getting actual jobs teaching or researching or brokering or some damn thing. The people who passed as my friends were from the bar and the games. I was uncomfortable at home, still restless in my thirties, which I assumed meant I always would be. And I drank too much.

During this time of my life I can't say with certainty what I wanted, but I know I was somewhere between going forward and going back. I craved newness, and I craved what had been. As I said, so many of my friends were gone, out there living lives that seemed true and real and together, if only to them. My ex-girl Julie-

Anne was among them. I was afraid, maybe, of either direction—becoming what I had always told people I wanted to be, and/or returning to the safety of school to try and fit into that mold that had once held me. And what resulted was a type of reckless malaise. I would live hard day to day. I would seek adventurous nights and heavy drink and hope to laugh hard once, even twice a day. The friends I had were card-room and barstool and wave-as-you-pass-by-me-in-the-hallway people mostly, and sometimes they seemed real, legitimate, because we talked about politics and books and getting laid and where we grew up and whether we hated our fathers or mothers worse. It could fool you, most of the time, but never fully. The life I was living then didn't completely seem like mine, it seemed like a close friend's, or one belonging to a secondary character in a film I'd once seen. It was an uncomfortable notion, when I thought about it. But, I didn't think about it all that often, and it *was* my life, no matter, so I pretty much had to keep living it and just see what went down next.

The prop bet was inevitable. We were all up in that little apartment a week after my "moment" with the girl, in-between hands. I remember I'd just won a big pot, and was pulling chips my way, beginning to stack them. The clatter and feel of the clay across my palms and fingertips made me feel like I'd be good, like everything would be okay. That feeling—if even for an instant—was what I played for.

When her light snapped on everyone went for the perch, leaving me stacking and the dealer saying something to me like, "Finally having a good night, Professor. Nice for you." That made me feel good, too.

When I got to the balcony she was already half undressed and a doughy shirtless guy stood in front of her swaying and doing some sort of embarrassing little sway-dance. She had, in the past, brought home athletic-looking, kind of classically handsome men. But this guy, it was clear, was not a handsome or athletic man, and comments were being made: "Dude, the girl is slumming it tonight," "Pillsbury should hire this motherfucker." Then Kenny chimed in that even Professor would be a better lay than this guy. Oooohs. Aaaaahs. And everyone looked my way, which was awkward, and halfway embarrassing. I mean, I considered myself decent looking—a little skinny and hook-nosed, but handsome in a tragic, tough-living old movie star capacity. I gave Kenny the finger and smiled, remained quiet for a while, just watched the show. She went down on the guy immediately, and right up against the window. Throughout the act there was a look of perfect pleasure and astonishment on this guy's face. I was jealous. Then I was hopeful. I started thinking hard about what Kenny had said. It was a moment of clarity. How did these people view me? What did they know of women I've had, books I've read, people I've loved, how I was spun-up and constantly worried about what next?

I don't know just why I said it, other than that I utterly believed it, but I pointed at Kenny and said, "I'll get this girl before any one of you assholes." I lit a cigarette and turned to watch the doughy guy pull up his pants and put on his shirt.

"A thousand dollars," Kenny said, sweeping his pointing finger in a half-circle. "No. Make it fifteen hundy. Me, or anyone else here gets her before you."

"You're putting up fifteen?" I said stepping toward him across the balcony. "I'll put up seven."

"Eight," Kenny said. "You get her, we'll put up fifteen. We get her, you put up eight. And it has to be here." He pointed to her apartment just as she slipped her robe on and followed the guy to the front door. "On a weekend night, right here for all of this."

"Deal." I reached out and shook his bony hand as the rest of them bobbed their heads and laughed like this should be a shit-barrel of fun.

Then we were back at the table, big pot after huge pot being won by everyone but me, and the prop bet wasn't really mentioned again. Maybe they thought it was a tawdry joke, or just another way I was going to feed them my tips and paycheck. But, it didn't come up, and that was fine because it was still a confirmed bet.

Days later I saw her around the corner from the bar. I was on my way to work, sitting to read the paper, smoke and drink coffee, but I had time, so I followed her. She was difficult to recognize at first, with those, or any, clothes on. She was very businesswoman—grey pantsuit, low heels, her red hair pinned up. But she had her stride, her mannerisms, and the way they were shadowed in my consciousness. I thought of the money, Kenny's handshake, and how I was going to get this done. I owed a thousand to the house now. I needed to get out from under it. I was so tired of owing. And now here she was. I was sure I could do this.

She sidled three blocks, and then slipped into a store that sold purses and luggage. She smelled like peaches mingled with all that leather.

Her name was Deanna, she told the clerk as I unzipped a suitcase or two. She had an accent—British or Australian or South African—which I should have recognized, and which endeared me to the task even further. Up close she wasn't nearly the beauty I, and the rest of us watchers, had assumed she must be. She was pretty beneath a layer of something awkward—a little bad skin, thin lips, a few cockeyed teeth. But she was tall, and put together well, and her eyes held a surety, an understanding that men would always be drawn to her. She bought what she needed, and I went off to work.

In the days following I saw her everywhere—walking near campus, playing tennis in the park, grocery shopping, talking business on a downtown street corner. And I watched her, or followed her—never too close, never for too long—and I had the sense that she knew, and that she liked it. A few nights later Deanna came into my bar and sat alone through two glasses of wine. I wasn't her server, but watched a couple of our regulars troll her table, sitting to talk and buy her another glass of Malbec. I was going to chat her up, too, but I choked, balked, and it all just seemed too awkward. Maybe, faced directly with this girl my context for pursuing her just seemed too silly and sleazy. Or, more likely, I hadn't been drinking enough yet that night. After my shift that night at the game, when we all saw her come home with a wiry kid in a cowboy hat, I vowed next time . . . next time, for sure.

—

A day later Julie-Anne showed up. I had had this girlfriend—Julie-Anne—a girl who'd been a student of mine when I was a teaching assistant. She'd since moved across the country to get her master's and Ph.D. She was very into learning, and for a time, very into me. We had been a minor scandal even though I only slept with her once when she'd been my student. Word got around, and for a minute or two I was looking at being kicked out of the program, or at least losing my TAship and funding. But, in the searchlight of philandering and infidelity other faculty members' skeletons were illuminated, and my hookup slipped from view.

She and I remained together for the year she was finishing up. Julie-Anne was a curious girl. She liked my dark side, my self-destructive side, my ability to seem comfortable while falling down. Julie-Anne. I always treated her and us like nothing big, a minor history. We drank, talked grandly about old wars and lost cities and human mythology, and we slept together—always knowing she'd be going to leave and go live a healthy, real life soon enough. It all allowed me to remain beyond love, or even loveliness. But, beneath our surface I knew there was more than I'd ever know what to do with.

So, Julie-Anne phoned to say she was coming through town. Could she stay with me on her way to Seattle where she was moving with her boyfriend who'd landed a job a month earlier. One night, she said, maybe two, and I said fine, I'm still in the same place, come find me.

Twenty minutes after Julie-Anne phoned there was someone

ringing my doorbell. In my boxers I opened the door to her standing with hands on hips. I shut the door, opened it again, and Julie-Anne gave me the finger and sneered her pouty lips. I opened my arms, showing my skinny bare chest, and said what the fuck?

"I was down at the gas station," she said. "My cell battery is dead."

"I thought you were driving in," I said. "Hours away."

"I didn't know I was going to call you," she said, "until I did."

"That makes a man feel right."

Julie-Anne stepped up and gave me a hug. She was a tall, almost frail girl. It had taken me a long time to get used to feeling her ribs and spine and hipbones, but I had, and now there on my porch, me in my boxers and staring bleary-eyed over her shoulder and out into the quiet weekday neighborhood, it was a little shock to wrap my arms so fully around her. I'd forgotten what it was like to hold a skinny thing like Julie-Anne. It felt good, new again.

"Come lie down with me," I said. "I still have sleeping to do."

"Jesus, Stephen, it's 11:00," Julie-Anne pushed at my chest, then followed me back inside.

I took her hand, saying, "I went to bed at dawn," kicking aside clothes, and bottles, and marked-up student essays—the detritus of my life—as we made our way to the bedroom's dim yellow light.

"I guess I drove pretty much all night." She sat on the bed's edge unbuttoning her jeans. "I could sleep."

I helped her lift off her t-shirt and scoot out of her jeans. We lay facing each other, then kissed tiredly, familiarly.

"Hello again." She smiled, setting her finger on my nose. "I'm moving to Seattle with a boy, you know."

"I know." I shut my eyes, smiling a little too. I turned her away from me, and hugged her, and soon enough we were both asleep.

When we woke that afternoon Julie-Anne wanted hamburgers and beer. It was the warm end of summer, and we sat outside at a neighborhood place we'd been dozens of times. After our first pitcher she told me about the Seattle dude, and after our second I started in on my debt and on how I was planning on getting out from under it. I told her all about the Deanna situation.

At first Julie-Anne didn't believe I'd do it, or that it was a good idea at all. "This is a human woman, Stephen," she said. "This is someone on my side of the species."

Then, as I explained the dark brilliance of it all, she leaned back on the worn wooden bench, smoking and looking me up and down. And she seemed to recapture the ridiculous draw I had to her. She drank off the rest of her beer, saying, "It's actually perfect, isn't it?"

"See," I said, pointing to my head. "You're back in this brain."

She made a gun with her pretty hand, shot herself in the head. She looked at the crowd of Lycra-draped mountain bikers who'd just rolled up. "I can think of better places to drink."

"I know a guy who's having a party."

"One of those school people? I can't go if it's one of those pretentious mud-stuck professor types."

"It's a guy from the bar." I stood. "It shouldn't be that much fun, but I want to show you off. They all think I only date fat chicks."

"That's a perfect reason."

"You look good. That's all I'm saying."

"Where can we find this Deanna?"

"She's out there." I swept my arm across the orange dusk sky. "In the ether of this city."

"I think we should get your money tonight. I think we can talk her into your bed."

"It has to be her bed," I said. "These people have to see this."

"Is this party walking distance?"

"Over by school. Staggering distance."

"I'm fine with it then," she said. "Let's go." And we went walking.

The party was worse than I thought. The host was the bouncer we'd just hired—a kid named Blake, or Davis, some preppy name that didn't fit his size and disposition. The rundown Victorian was filled with loud kids wearing cargo shorts and polos, like our bouncer. He high-fived both Julie-Anne and me when we stepped through the door—"Stephen, the mother-fucking Professor," he said, reaching high above our heads, "this is a not a fat chick." Clutches of college kids performed keg stands and recited bad movie quotes and shaky pick-up lines on Julie-Anne. I was happy to find the liquor and pour us keg cups full of gin and lemonade which cut the beery heat and strangeness of seeing Julie-Anne again, and telling her about Deanna and my shitty little debt, and how it was to still be a guy like me bringing her to a shit party like this. But Julie-Anne seemed to like the boys' attention, at least for a little while, which was her way. So I went out into the sprawling backyard to smoke and drink within the maple tree shadows.

I watched my students wander in and out of the hazy rooms, lit it up gold and red. As my buzz came on I felt old and contemplative as I shifted into an understanding that I'd never know the answers to my life's questions, though sometimes I would believe I did.

After a time my very favorite former student, a kid named Moses, found me back there sitting on a low branch. Moses was a thick, loud kid—though somehow different than this crowd. He was wise in a common, earnest way, and I admired him for it, even if he fit in perfectly here and nearly everywhere I saw him—the college bars and cafes and parties like this one. The one class Moses took from me he'd stopped showing halfway through the term, only to emerge the last week with slides of his month-long trip to Amsterdam. He asked me if he could show the class a slide show of what he'd gone and done, said a lecture I'd given inspired him to hit his rich uncle up for cash and take the trip into the wide world while he could. I gave him an A as long as he promised not to tell anyone or brag about what he'd gotten away with.

"Prof," he said, slipping into the shadows, cupping my hand in his meaty fingers. "I have something for you."

Moses handed me a little baggie. "Hash. From my trip. I brought back a whole little load of it. Down here." He pointed to his crotch, and rubbed at his ass.

"Really." I sipped at my drink, looked hard up into Moses' squinty red eyes. "That's a long, sweaty flight."

"I've been waiting to smoke you out, Prof," he said, nodding his big stubbly face. "I couldn't give it to you during the semester."

"I'm good now, too." I handed him back the baggie, and shook the ice in my keg cup. "Cocktails suit me fine."

"Shit," Moses said, "I guess that's more for me."

"More for you, my friend. Smoke up, and then we'll go mix another big drink, or two."

"You're always full of good ideas, Prof," Moses said, and got himself a little higher.

Inside, near the kitchen keg circle Moses and I found Julie-Anne demonstrating how to perform The Running Man for the boys. The room was dank, smelling of overripe fruit and patchouli. I made another big cocktail, and Julie-Anne smoked what Moses offered, and soon enough we were marching toward downtown beneath the warm light of streetlamps and stars.

Sometime later we saw her, Deanna, sitting in the deep-yellow light of a windowed corner bar right downtown. She was alone, sitting on a brushed-aluminum barstool, fingering the stem of a martini glass, leaning over the bar and laughing with the bartender, a little balding guy whose name was Andrew. I knew him from around. I'd sat right there and laughed like that with him, too, and it made me feel both hopeful and sad to stand on that warm corner and watch Deanna toss her head back, run fingers through her tight-curled hair. There were three guys sitting at the bar listening to the lilt of that accent, thinking they could take home something like her. They looked like others I'd seen from our side of the alley, and I stood there with my hands shoved deep into my pockets thinking, yes, tonight's the night.

Julie-Anne and Moses walked half a block before they realized I'd stopped to gawk amongst the drunken kids milling up and down the gum-spotted sidewalks, eating street-vender hotdogs and gyros.

"Prof?" Moses stepped to my side, setting his heavy hand on my head.

Julie-Anne came ambling up and grabbed my ass. "It's not a museum, buddy."

I put my hand on Julie-Anne's. "That's her," I said. "There she sits."

"Who are you ogling?" Moses said.

Julie-Anne squinted through the window, and we both took a step closer to Deanna who was now eyeballing one particular fellow down at the end of the bar. I was jealous, scared, perfectly excited.

"The alley girl?" Julie-Anne said. "The payoff girl?"

"None other."

Moses said, "Take a picture, Prof. You can whack off at home."

"Let me explain this to you, Mr. Moses." Julie-Anne turned to him and lit into an abbreviated and spiced-up version of the Deanna story—one in which much more money was at stake, one in which my sexual prowess bordered on the legendary. Julie-Anne was excellent at making me sound like the king of *something*. Moses nodded and nodded, and when she finished he said, "I guess we have a new place to drink."

"We do," I said, leading them through the door.

—

Julie-Anne took me into the women's room and fussed with my hair and wiped my face with a wet paper towel. "Let's get the shine off your pretty face," she said. "Let's get this collar straightened."

"Pretty face?" I squinted at my ruddy face in the mirror. "You have eye drops?"

"We're going to get this job done," she said, then reached her hands around my neck, pulled me to her, and kissed me. Then I took her hand and led us back to the bar. Julie-Anne whispered, "Talk about the Spanish Inquisition, the Emancipation Proclamation. Talk about the sacking of Rome."

"That *always* works." I leaned my head back, dropping a cool rain of Visine across my eyes.

"Worked on me."

At the bar beside Deanna, I ordered a Boodles martini, and watched Andrew do his quick, clean work, clattering and shaking and sifting ice and gin. There was a low murmuring amidst the house music, and the back-lit bar seeped diamond blue and a bright lemon yellow behind the bottles. Deanna smelled like soap and sage as I leaned closer to her bare shoulder.

She slowly turned my way, cocked her head and smiled, showing a crooked incisor. "Hello?"

"You smell like something brand new." I smiled back.

"Thank you," she said, "I think?"

"It's a good thing, yes. I meant it that way."

She reached across and touched my forearm, leaning in and

smelling my neck. "Your smell is more like something gently used, but still nice."

Her accent bowed in the air between us, even when she laughed, and we moved easily into conversation and drink in a way that surprised me. She told me about a trip she took as a girl to Tasmania. I told her I was either getting my doctorate, or becoming a professional poker player, or training to be a motivational speaker. I put the drinks on my nearly-maxed Discover card.

"Don't go anywhere," I told Deanna. "I command you to stay put."

Deanna smiled, nodded, and sat at the bar putting on lipstick as I went to find Julie-Anne and Moses.

They were outside the bar's front door eating hot dogs.

"This is going well," I told them. "I almost wish it was more of a challenge."

"I told you," Julie-Anne said, her mouth full, Moses nodding behind her. "You are the pants-off charmer."

"I am the sans-pants king," I said, then took her by the shoulders and explained in detail how to get to the poker apartment, explained how she had to get everyone out on the patio, how they had to promise that the act was payment in full. Then I called Kenny the houseman and told him Julie-Anne and Moses were coming over shortly. He said fine, send them, and then I was back at Deanna's side signing for the drinks and taking her hand to lead her out into the night.

—

Near 2am Deanna had a hold of my belt and was pulling me across her apartment's threshold, tumbling us in a slow-motion twist of boozy flesh and rumpled fabric onto her polished hardwood entryway. She had her mouth against my belly and was saying something about American boys, kissing and licking and moaning in a manner she thought was very sexy. Her slurred accent made her sound like a Muppet now, that trippy blonde one who plays guitar in the band with Animal. This all put me off a little and though I was certainly drunk, letting her go to work, I began to feel acutely sober, sharp, contemplative in a manner that made me reconsider what the hell I was doing there at all. For a moment I thought about leaving. But, I realized, as we untangled and stood in the dim and spice-fragrant kitchen, that this was a stupid drunken reverie. I'd had enough of them to know that I should ignore it all.

"I'm taking a shower, Mr. Good Bloke, sir." Deanna led me into the living room where the bottles and candles and matching blue-velvet couch and loveseat stared at me and said, Well it's about fucking time, bud. Deanna tugged at my belt again. "I think you should join. I think we should get wet together."

"I've had my shower," I said, wondering if Moses and Julie-Anne had made it to the poker apartment, thinking how I couldn't risk finishing this job out of view, back in the shower. "I'm a clean, clean bloke."

"Not too clean." She unbuttoned her blouse. "I hope."

"I've never been that."

In an instant she was naked, but for a magenta thong, and

strutting into the back room where I heard her start up the shower and begin humming. It all seemed a show, I thought, and wondered what films this woman had taken her cues from—*Body Heat, 9 ½ Weeks, Top Gun?*—or, if this was just her way. Or, maybe I was just not a movie sex type of guy. Maybe I was just a drink-and-grope guy, maybe I was just a lights-off-and-rut guy. I'd never considered this fully. Leaning against her couch, smelling some kind of orange peel and thyme potpourri, running my finger over the dust of a framed-up *Starry Night* print.

I unbuttoned my own shirt and for some reason took off my shoes and socks, then made for the deck. The night was still and warm. Lights were on in the poker apartment behind blinds. I squinted up against them trying to see Julie-Anne, or Moses, or anyone at all who was willing to bare witness up on that deck and watch me pick my way through this business.

"Stephen," Julie-Anne hissed. "How's it going?"

"Julie-Anne?" I shout-whispered back. "I have my shoes off, and my socks."

"Where's the girl?"

"Showering." I lit a cigarette, hip-thrusting against the railing. "Getting ready for the ride."

"Please, Stephen. That sounds like something these fuckers would say."

"They're all there? They're all ready?"

"It took me a minute to convince them that you had this figured out. Moses helped tell it right."

"And they agreed to the terms?"

"You get it done." She looked back towards the patio door as it swung open. "You're debt-free. Plus 500 to the good side."

Moses stepped up beside her, swaying. "Prof, I already lost three hundred. Had to go the ATM. This is shark-infested water, bro."

"Five minutes," I said, as the shower water cut out behind me and Deanna's off-key singing got louder. "Gather the voyeurs."

She and Moses applauded lightly, and I slipped back inside to find Deanna leaning against the kitchen counter pouring glasses of white wine. "It's from New Zealand." She turned to hand me a glass, her silky yellow robe falling open to show clean pink breasts and hips. "Fucking Kiwis."

"Fucking Kiwis." I took the glass and toasted.

In the middle of everything I was certain I could hear barks and catcalls from across the alley. Deanna had taken hold of my head from the start, forcing it down and between and behind and up again, and the astonished and crass voices of those players, those fucking sharks, the gasps of Julie-Anne and Moses, all rang and echoed through my skull, mingling with the histrionic moaning of Deanna. I listened and pushed instinctually, not certain whether I was enjoying myself or not. And I don't know how long it lasted—ten minutes? twenty days? as long as it took me to lose that $1,500? the haunted rest of my life?

While I was naked me, pushing around in that golden candle-light, in that perfumed little space, I just thought about the task, how it was to finally meet a goal, how it was to provide entertainment and astonishment, how I was finally, if temporarily, debt-free and unmoored. I became some sort of twisted little hero, to myself at least.

I can't say if I was good. But I don't think I was bad, at least not inept. I moved around as she wanted, I was in and out, I got the condom on first try. I let her finish (at least in theory) first. I lay and stroked my hand gently down her inner thigh in the awkward "afterglow" as she rolled over and said in a happy drunken manner, "So good." Then she was after another glass of wine, and sing-songing that she was going to bathe.

"You just had a shower, sister," I said, lying on the floor, cupping a hand over my crotch.

She looked at me quite seriously, up and down. "I know," she said, "but . . .you know."

"Not really."

"Just lie there," she said, "relax."

I did lie there. I pulled her yellow robe over me, reposed there watching light lurch across the walls and ceiling, then I rolled over and tried to squint through the sliding-glass door and up at the poker balcony. All I could see was my bleary, shadowed reflection. I wasn't quite ready to go out there and see who was making brilliant jokes at my expense, or what Julie-Anne thought about it all, so I lay still and shut my eyes.

Sometime later—seconds? days?—sirens and bursting red-blue light filled the air. It took me a long moment to remember just where I was, but the Van Gogh print reflecting those urgent colors brought Deanna's voice and soft pink body right back. Where was she? And what was going on out in the alleyway? I stood up fast, slipping into Deanna's silky yellow robe. Then I was on the balcony staring down at an aide car and paramedics talking low as they crouched over a prone body. A small crowd huddled at the periphery. Up at the poker apartment players and house men and dealers leaned over the rail. I waved and asked what's up, but no one seemed to notice me. I pulled the robe tight, then yelled, "Hey, Julie-Anne! Hey Moses!"

"Oh shit," some cloaked figure on the deck said, "check out the Professor." Several of them pointed.

Then from the alley came, "Stephen! Oh man, Stephen!" I couldn't see Julie-Anne until she stepped out of the huddle beside the aide car.

"What?" I shrugged and spread my arms. "What the fuck?!"

Julie-Anne stared up at me, standing silent for a moment, palms pressed hard to her cheeks. A couple of other residents in Deanna's building had come out to their lanais. I shouted questions at them, but they all ignored me standing there in that soft, flowery robe. Down below people were murmuring, "Oh man. Damned unbelievable. Oh hell."

"What are you doing?" I shouted down to Julie-Anne. "And did you see me do the deed? I got it done. I got it finished."

"It's Moses," she said, stepping across the alley and just below me. Her brow was knit tight. She pointed. "He's on the asphalt over there."

"I'll be down," I said. "Don't move from there."

"He's hurt."

—

Deanna was passed out in the bathtub. More candles were lit, and a few bath-beads were spilled on the tub's rim. I stood above her marveling at the smooth shape of her pale-pink skin, the wash of red pubic hair, wondering if there was any possible way she'd remember me among the litany.

The bath water was still warm as I reached for her, thinking to wake her up. But, I pulled back, went to find my clothes, then walked through the apartment blowing out all the candles, feeling proud of my conscientiousness. I left her slightly snoring in that cooling water.

In the alley I found Julie-Anne peering over the shoulders of the U-shaped crowd watching the paramedics work. They had Moses on a flat-board, and seemed to be delicately checking his vitals. He had a long, angry scrape across his face and neck, and was smiling as he mouthed words into the warm night. As they hoisted him into the ambulance he gave us all the thumbs up. Julie-Anne took my arm and led me down the alley.

"It was in the middle of everything," she started. "We had everyone gathered, and you were both pretty much naked."

"Did I do good? Was I impressive?"

"I don't know," she said. "Yes. Probably."

"Are they paying? Am I good with them?"

"Will you quit with the bet, with the girl?" She squeezed my arm hard. "Moses is hurt over there."

"He looked okay, Julie-Anne," I said. "He was smiling."

"I don't think so," she said, and lit into just what Moses had done.

He'd been very excited about all of it, and when Deanna and I had come sauntering into the living room, groping and thrusting, Moses made for the railing, pushing a couple of the regular players aside so he could get the ideal view. He kept murmuring, "Wow, Prof. Go, Prof! Wow, Prof!" The guys started telling him to step aside, to let the lady up front, to shut up for a minute.

"He did," Julie-Anne said. "He just kind of went quiet and invisible. I forgot about him for a while, and I just leaned over and watched you guys. It was like a perverted science class, or something. It made me think about what I look like, what you and me maybe look like, doing that business. Then. Then I see him cartwheeling through the air. Moses. Right there." She reached her trembly hand all the way out, wiping at the air. "He fell. Or jumped. Or something, something happened. I think he climbed up to the roof to get a view. And he shit and fuck fell, Stephen."

"Three floors?" I said. "All the way?"

"He caught the tree." She came in close to hug me. Down the alley the aide car slowly pulled away, and the little crowd began to dissipate, some of them making their way back up to the game, some just wandering back into the night. "Branches snapped. Then . . . thud."

"He's a big man."

"Do you really think he's okay?"

I looked up at the poker balcony, then up toward Deanna's place. No one was visible at all. And the alley was empty but for a guy in an electric wheelchair slowly rolling by at the far end. It all seemed a tiny nightmare, but somehow not my own. I wondered at my role in it.

We decided to walk to Saint Luke's, fifteen blocks down. I figured this is where they'd taken Moses, but when we got there and stood in the bright florescence of the ER asking where he was they said no, nobody named Moses had been admitted tonight.

"Maybe that's not his real name." I was looking over at Julie-Anne, then the nurse. "Big guy, though. Fell off a roof."

"We can't give out information," the bone-skinny little nurse said, "but no, he's not here. Try Saint Al's, up the hill. They have the better trauma center."

"We can't walk that far." Julie-Anne began to cry. "We can't walk that far, Stephen. I'm so fucking tired, Stephen. Tired."

"He'll be all right, Julie-Anne," I said, nodding. "All this is fine. If somebody can call us a cab, we'll be okay."

"Who'll be with him?"

"Someone," I said. "Someone will."

So we sat waiting in the white light beneath the ER's portal, but the called-for cab never materialized, or maybe we got impatient, or forgot why we were there at all. We walked home, to my apartment, and never went to find Moses. We lay on my sofa and drank half the bottle of wine Julie-Anne had brought as a token, and she made me take a long shower before we got into bed and slept through until three in the afternoon.

———

I never got to know if anyone was there at St. Al's with Moses when he died. And I have never told Julie-Anne that he died at all. She drove out that next evening, looking frayed and urgent and a little sad that she had stopped in on me at all.

"Something's always messed up around you, Stephen." She leaned against her Saab.

"I'm glad you were here for it this time around." I kissed her on the mouth, but she didn't kiss me back.

She'd wanted to go to the hospital on her way out, thought it was the right thing. But, I convinced her to just go, just drive out into the new life. When she phoned from a ferry boat skimming across Elliott Bay three weeks later I told her Moses was fine, and that I was fine, and that the night before when I'd taken him out for a "recovery" drink he'd asked about her and about why the hell I hadn't stuck with such a fine one when I had the chance.

I didn't tell her the truth of the matter at all, how I'd taken a cab up to St. Al's to check on Moses that evening she'd left—a lonely Sunday night in the ER, the white fluorescents humming, one or two invalids rolling the hallways. I didn't tell Julie-Anne how I'd told the head nurse that I was a close friend of Moses', and a former teacher. I didn't say how, this nurse, she looked so fucking guilty when she stood, came to the other side of her clean beige desk, leaned close to my ear and said, "Too much bleeding," touching at her head. "He's gone . . . we lost him . . . this afternoon."

"He didn't die," I said, but she nodded yes, he did.

I didn't tell Julie-Anne about my little knee buckle, or the bile that rose to the back of my throat, or the cold tremble in my thighs that rose into my shoulders and head. I didn't tell her how I walked out of the ER and then the miles to the poker apartment downtown—numb and sad and smoking Camel after Camel—but that no one was there in that apartment at all, that the door was open and that it was empty, hollow, the tables and chairs and chips and mini-bar all removed to show a stained-up blue shag. I didn't tell her how I'd sat down in that little space and tried without success to cry, or how I'd gone out to the deck and watched Deanna read her little book of poetry or god-words, wearing that dumb yellow robe like a costume. I didn't tell Julie-Anne how the Moses incident had spooked the guys who ran the game, or how they'd moved the operation to a little warehouse space near the fair grounds and had the game running the very next night. I didn't tell her how I'd taken a cab out there the night before, or that I'd lied to them too about Moses being fine, or that I was back in debt a few hundred again already. I didn't tell her about the funeral I'd been planning to attend, but which I slept through.

I just walked with the phone out to my front steps. It was a cloudless, midday with no wind. The August light was hazy, and everything seemed tired. I lit a cigarette with slightly fluttering hands, then eased the cherry close to my wrist. My eyes watered against the pain, and my heart sped, and I sat silently as I listened to Julie-Anne laugh and ask me if I could hear the waves rolling into side of the ferryboat, or the gulls screeching above, or the tinny PA announcement saying they'd be docking any minute.

I bit hard at my cheek, tasting blood, remaining quiet for a long moment before, "Hello?" Julie-Anne said. "Stephen? Are you still with me? Can you hear any of this?"

MAP OF CALIFORNIA

When you ask me if we'll ever make it out of California the blood is up in my mouth and fracture is in our ears. We're driving north through the Central Valley at the end of summer. Windows down, and nothing but Reno ahead. It's all agriculture and a cloudless sky and us trying to outrun the life we lost on the coast. That all seems a decade ago—Big Sur, Pismo Beach—but it was only last month. Now we're trying to figure out how we fucked up that beauty, too. The black rock tide pools and the bonfires and the canned beer and the one thing coming into another and the songs and the blank mind of morning and the collection of sand along the seam and the salt and the elephant seals and starfish and all of us trying to be one thing without asking for permission and the two of us trying to memorize each others' lives. Here, it's acres of cattle and all of America's produce framing the interstate. We stop for Mexican food in Turlock where out front you call your brother from the last payphone in the west. He'll be meeting us in Carson City by dusk. I'll drive into Nevada without you. Another life hunches out there, waiting. We will seek it alone. In the dry afternoon I touch your thin arm, your ribcage and neck, just to say thank you, good-bye. On the table inside I unfold the map, but then the food comes too quick and the plates are too hot and you bow your head as if you are praying, but that's not it, not at all.

ROUGH CUT

The Mormon has fought before. Tompkins sees this right off and it scares him, his belly clenching at the ribs as he watches Bean absorb gut-shots and jabs from the Mormon, a man they have never seen. Tompkins leans against the concrete wall abutting the vacant lot and stagnant summer creek, the thin hair on his arms laying sun-bright over tightening skin. The Mormon is putting it to Bean, tearing his uniform shirt, biting at his shoulder, landing three blows to Bean's one as they tumble across the oil-mottled corner of the parking lot behind Lowry's Discount Tire out Fairview, in Boise, where Tompkins and Bean work the back yard full-time.

This man has fought in crooked alleyways, Tompkins thinks, in vacant lots, in woeful heat or rampant cold. He's fought where baited air hangs like rot. The Mormon is smooth, direct, a dirty fighter. Feet shuffling like a rough-cut boxer, scratching at the pavement, he spits, purses his thin lips, and takes what he needs from Bean without recognizing doubt or disgust. A man fueled by instinct, Tompkins believes, a man born with desires he has tried to outrun.

Tompkins listens to the grunts and tussle, listens to the heavy traffic up Fairview where men and women roll and lurch in autos, in trucks, air-conditioned and unaware of his watching, his inept leaning. Bean is bleeding, and Tompkins stands still.

"You go in," Bean has told Tompkins. "Go right the hell into a fight. Strike. Shock the man, take something, before he hurts you."

"Right," Tompkins said. "Yes."

It was the second day they met, Bean explaining yellow bruises across his neck, Tompkins listening, feeling his insides flutter, whir.

"That's how I whip ass," Bean said. "Alone. Believe it. I do it alone."

Now it's turned upside down, and Tompkins, afraid for Bean, thinks, I am a statue while my only friend is being beaten. Tompkins aches to step in, but has never fought. He's heard all about it from Bean, but has never drawn a fist, let it fly toward another man, doesn't know if he could. Tompkins would love to be like Bean—fearless, bent—but he is shorter, pale and small, so drawn to the fight, but unable, he believes, to carry out the intrigue.

The Mormon looks like the others Tompkins has seen all summer—the smooth-skinned boys in white shirts and plain ties, missionaries, half-smiling, peaceful as they walk Fairview up beyond the Big and Tall, down past the Food Warehouse. The Mormon boys want someone to talk with, to impart what they know, and they seek them out, strolling over the rubble—cigarette butts and spent condoms, singular shoes, underwear, half-eaten cheeseburgers—the chaff Tompkins himself sees each day. These weeks since he and his mother moved, Tompkins has intently watched the Mormons—pairs of boys looking so much younger than he who is eighteen, or Bean who now is twenty.

Bean moves in, casting a white fist that glances the Mormon's neck. The Mormon dodges, ducks, and he counters, connects, a shot to Bean's chest that sounds like a deep drum beat.

Tompkins leers at the swaying men—Bean bleeding above his left eye, the Mormon circling, stalking. Breath whorling, weighty, their clenched fists try to out-do gravity—rise high, drop hard. Bean says, "fucker" "pissant" "lemming." The Mormon says nothing, just pants, wrenches at his tie, throws it aside in a weightless arc, and again charges Bean fast with a low shoulder and quickening eyes, eyes believing in nothing but this sharp blue moment.

Tompkins and his mother came from Seattle in June. She picked him up the last day of senior classes, and they drove east in the Skylark his father left them when he moved south and away four years ago. Tompkins only had one peripheral friend—a junior who called herself Frank, a mousy girl who after school played gin rummy and walked the neighborhoods near school with Tompkins, talking about her plans to work and travel and expertly know the world. He didn't get to say goodbye to Frank, didn't in fact know he and his mother were leaving that day until they were down I-5 and ramping east onto I-90. It was a long ride to Boise for Tompkins, who sat sullen and angry beside his mother as she smoked her long brown cigarettes and explained that it was an emergency, that they were three months late on rent, that his father and his support money were nowhere to be found. She had a plan, she said. They were going to Boise, moving in with a man she knew, a friend named Mikey. She reached across the console to squeeze Tompkins' wrist. "He's a decent man," she said, smiling wide, showing the thin wrinkles at her eyes and mouth. "People like him. We call him Thin Mikey. He's real tall honey. You can call him that, too." She let go of his wrist, whispering, "This will all work out fine. Absolutely fine."

Tompkins felt adrift, meaningless, watching the yellow evening sky darken above the open land east of Yakima. If only he could have said goodbye, given Frank a handshake or a kiss.

Thin Mikey, his skin deeply tanned from time spent greenskeeping at the city golf course, was taciturn and almost kind. He stood over Tompkins as he ate breakfast in the cramped, blue-painted kitchen that first morning, and told him he drank with a businessman named Lowry, that he would pull strings, help get him a job.

"You better start holdin' your own now, buddy," Thin Mikey said. "You live in my house, you work. Got it champ?"

"Sure," Tompkins said, "I guess so," captured, looking into the charming, wry smile of Thin Mikey, held by the surety of his presence. Tompkins hated Thin Mikey hard because he saw why his mother had changed into her red leather skirt before they pulled into Boise, why her voice rose and trilled when Thin Mikey said, "Look at you, Terri," then hugged her as she stepped from the Skylark and into his arms.

Tompkins was trained for the grunt job of tire stacker and go-fer by Bean, who has worked at Lowry's for two years, and who took to Tompkins, began telling him so many things he hadn't known. Bean has eyes like Tompkins has never seen, eyes like wishing stars. Bean is tall and lithe with sugar-blond hair, and his words have a presence. Stories fall from Bean. This man has lived.

Tompkins knew it right off, listening to Bean retell his seducing of three girls in one night at a party in the orchards. Bean has told Tompkins how he stood up to his own father, kicked his ass real good when he was only fifteen, how his daddy moved out because he was afraid of Bean. Tompkins has sat quietly as Bean's whispered tales of drinking at the High Low Bar down Fairview, where they've been letting him shoot tequila, play pool, and juke-box dance since his senior year at Capital High. He has watched Bean's long fingers wrap up old tires with gallant strength, with grace.

"You'll see them," Bean has said. "Mormons trooping down Fairview. They like to think we need saving."

"Mormonville," Tompkins said. "That's what Mom calls it."

"They'll come to your house," Bean said. But, Tompkins has only seen them walking Fairview looking feckless, so weak, peeking into windows of Confucius Chinese Buffet, of Wendy's.

Now Bean and the Mormon circle, and Tompkins balances on one foot, whispering, "Punch, Bean. Swing. Act what you know." Tompkins wants so badly to step in, wants to save Bean from disgrace and pain, but his feet are leaden, hot anchors in the broken afternoon. Tompkins watches closely, listens, solving pieces of the fast-spinning world. Bean is wincing. A plane traces a contrail across the brightest sky. Bean is a staggering wayward idol. Men on that plane are going to London, or Sri Lanka, places they have never been. The smell of diesel is creeping in from the rumbling trucks up Fairview. The Mormon is so quiet, so strong. Where did he learn this?

He is base and hateful, not weak. A troubled vessel, Tompkins thinks, though he couldn't see it as the Mormon approached he and Bean, alone, straight-faced, grasping a Bible, wearing a back-pack. Bean hates them, has always hated them. Bean has wanted to fuck one up, and he taunted this man with talk of sacrilege and po-lygamy as he has with others who have wandered through the lot to find he and Tompkins stacking used tires in the disposal truck. Bean was telling a story about Sally Beecher, his long-legged sum-mer girl, a woman who has touched places, he said to Tompkins, he hadn't even known existed.

"Porno horny, Tompkins," Bean said. "She wraps me up and breathes the crazy shit in my ears."

"Damn," Tompkins said, and he saw the Mormon ease across the lot. "Here comes a white shirt."

"It's *Bean yes, Bean do me, Bean Bean Bean.*"

"Hello," the Mormon said. "Can I talk with you, about some-thing important?"

"Go find your own place in hell," Bean said, stepping to the Mormon. "This is ours." He gave him the finger, knocked the Bi-ble from his hands, turned and walked, winking at Tompkins. Bean expected him to walk, to just go as they have all summer, heads held up, hands in the pockets of rumpled trousers. Tompkins saw rage gather in the Mormon as his eyes landed on Bean's.

"I've had Mormon girls," Bean said, hip-thrusting, giddy. "A planet of 'em."

The Mormon set his backpack down and charged Bean hard. Bean never expected it, and now the rap of fist landing on skin levels in Tompkins' ears.

Sometimes Tompkins is curious, wishes Bean would lay off, let them draw he and Bean into their calm, neatly-folded way. It may be easier, may hold the curious numbness Tompkins desires as he walks the avenue, watching, listening with exactitude and purpose each morning, each evening—five quiet and dirty blocks between Lowry's and Thin Mikey's place.

"Jackass," Bean says, tiptoe backpedaling, nodding, grinning at Tompkins to say, okay. I'm okay. "You think you hurt me?"

The Mormon stands in the middle of Bean's showy pugilist's circle, stands smiling at Bean, a wicked smile, frigid and brave. Tompkins digs into his pockets, finds a matchbook, and lights a cigarette from Bean's pack, smokes deeply, so anxious for Bean. He hears men laughing, coughing in the bay of the Discount Tire. He hears the hum of the hydraulic lift as Bean and the Mormon for one moment stand still. A car honks in the bay, its shallow echo loud, exact. Tompkins swallows hard. His eyes water.

He's seen Bean take on all comers this summer, egg on more, and Tompkins loves him for this. Bean has long muscles tight across the six-foot-two of him, and he is strong, so much stronger than he looks. Tompkins only knows him to belt vital men to the pavement. Yet, today he looks misshapen.

"Watch that Bean," Thin Mikey's told Tompkins. "He's loose with his words. I've seen him at the High Low. He comes at things too hard."

"He's tough as shit," Tompkins said. "He's a lion."

"You just watch him," Thin Mikey said. "The boy's not all you think he is. No boy is. Your daddy wouldn't let Bean in the house. You're daddy would smack your head just for thinking Bean's the type of man you wanna be."

"Dad ain't around here though, is he? Besides, I thought you hated my daddy. Besides, Bean'd whip my daddy," Tompkins said. And Thin Mikey walked, shaking his long slow head.

Today, Tompkins thinks, look at Bean fall, watch the Mormon make him look like a wrong thing.

The Mormon—rounded and shorter, his hair course and straw-blond—keeps fighting in a steep, rugged fashion and Bean has no chance. "Go get married again," Bean shouts, and the Mormon lunges, reaches with thick hands and ranging forearms, broad muscles arcing elbow to wrist. He wraps Bean up, holding him to the shaded concrete beside the dumpster. Bean can't move, the Mormon has him pinned, right cheek to the asphalt. Bean is winded, heaving breath for what seems minutes as resignation creeps in and he appears sad, quickly unfamiliar, looking to Tompkins for help. Tompkins remains still, hoping it is over, hoping that the man will let Bean up, let Bean curse him, send him back into the hot concrete landscape.

The Mormon, though, is not finished. He pushes Bean's head, twisting his cheek into the grit. He begins butting, enraged. Head-butting, spit spraying from his clenched teeth, a low grunt comes louder with each thrust.

"Enough," Tompkins says, but the Mormon keeps it up, and Bean begins to scream.

"Jesus Christ." Tompkins runs at the Mormon. "Shit Jesus!" He lurches forward, knocking the Mormon free of Bean with a leap, a tackle, feeling a distant weight dart in close, merge with his own, and bound away. Bean rolls out of the Mormon's reach, presses a palm to his forehead, pulling it away to see a sticky bright patch of red. Bean sucks air through his teeth as he stands, looks at the Mormon above Tompkins now, shaking his head, still silent. The Mormon is dirty, smudged with gray oil and dusty blood, but unhurt—maybe one scrape, two, but nothing like Bean. It will take Bean weeks to look right again. Tompkins sees the Mormon above him, and in his eyes the trouble is retreating. He's folding it up, Tompkins thinks, tucking the anger back inside.

"Don't," Tompkins says, as the Mormon crouches, shoves his chest lightly, turning to let the fight sit behind him while he picks up his tie, his bag, his Bible. Holding them he walks away, turning once to wave his wide middle finger as Bean shouts, "God? Fuck God! You think you know anything about heaven's high reward? Fuck you."

Tompkins stands, tight-chested, unsure, feeling a fragmented sympathy for Bean who looks weak, twisted up. I have helped him, he thinks, Bean needed me.

—

Behind the vined cyclone fence, the summer creek runs slow and murky. Tompkins helps Bean creep over the low concrete wall and through a cut hole in the fence to sit beside the creek. They say nothing, though Tompkins wants to ask: "What will Sally Beecher say? What will Thin Mikey tell me about fucking with the unknown? Did you really whip your father?" But, these aren't right questions, and Tompkins waits for Bean to speak. Respect for the defeated, he thinks, plus, he may not be the same Bean. "A sound beating will shrink a man," Thin Mikey's told him. "Separate him from his true self."

The afternoon is so silent. Tompkins can just feel Bean tremble beside him as they sit and dangle their legs above the creek. The water looks rigid, unmovable to Tompkins who sets his hand on Bean's left knee. Round, warbling music, bass-driven and primal, slips through the air coming off Fairview, air smelling of hot engines, stale rubber. Tompkins feels Bean breathe, and he lets his hand linger, waiting for Bean to say something bright and wise, waiting for Bean to pull his leg away.

In the creek are two pizza boxes, half-submerged. There are minnows darting, and sun-faded cola cans, water-skippers, a computer keyboard, the brown-green reflection of an empty sky and crooked tree branches reaching, reflections of the boot soles of Bean and Tompkins. Bean puts his hand on Tompkins', taps a finger, and a measured half-smile creases Bean's face.

"Buddy, he fucked me up good," Bean says.

Tompkins pulls back his hand, looks up at Bean, smiling and

swollen. "Yeah," he says. "Yeah he did." And he holds Bean's stare. "Guess no more work today."

"Thanks for waiting," Bean says. "Before saving my ass." He spits blood and white saliva into the creek, and minnows rise through the quick ripple to peck the oblong spot.

"I'm sorry."

"No," Bean says. "Serious."

"You're not," Tompkins pauses. "I don't know, I couldn't move. I didn't want to embarrass you. I'm sorry."

"You moved. Besides, that fucker was tough."

"Yeah," Tompkins says. He turns, sees that the back lot of Lowry's is still and empty. "Is he the toughest guy you ever fought?"

"Fucking Mormon," Bean says. "Of all the goddamned things. Am I still bleeding?"

Tompkins raises his hand to Bean's head, touches a raw spot above his ear, gently lets blood collect on his thumb and pulls it away to show Bean. "Some," he says. Tompkins points to black bugs skittering the surface over clouds of algae. "Can you believe anything lives in there?"

Bean nods, "Water walkin' Jesus Bugs."

Tompkins nods back, surprise lighting in his chest as he eyes the bright contrast of Bean's red blood on his own gray, dirt-smudged skin.

"There was a guy I fought in school," Bean says. "A guy named Douglass Birr, before you and your mom moved here. Douglass Birr, I fought him because he was a liar and I thought I hated liars. He lied all the time—about girls, money, a stamp collection he never owned, a trip to Japan his family never made. He was a liar, everybody'd known it since the first grade. People hated him for the lies, but they were nice to him 'cause they wanted to hear what would come out next. They liked making fun of him so much that they talked to him, let him pull as much shit out of his ass as he could, just so they could pass it along.

"I always felt a little sorry for him. He was a nice enough dude. But, one day he started telling people that he saw me stealing baseball cards from K-Mart, stuffing 'em down my pants and walking out. I knew I had to fight him. Had to."

"You beat his ass?" Tompkins feels Bean's blood dry on the contour of his thumb. As Bean talks, looking across the creek and the dry weed field, over the cinderblock wall to the black-shingled rooftops that lie beyond, Tompkins brings his thumb to his mouth and tastes Bean's blood. Salt and sweat. The red rumble of Bean. He tastes it, tastes it, wants the red rumble of Bean. It dissolves across his palette—lingers, pulses—and Tompkins remembers Thin Mikey's breath, his sullen words coming in close, slow and angry words stacking up, and he wishes he had it in him to stand and face a man like Thin Mikey, curse him, shove him, no matter.

"Douglass Birr kicked my ass sideways," Bean says. "We fought in the park, all alone, and he kicked the tar out of me."

"I thought you never lost," Tompkins says, biting his thumb, thinking to pierce it, mix in his own blood.

"That's what I always say because shit, Birr never told anyone. You know that next day at school I told people I fell off my dirt bike, and Birr went along with it. I think he liked the lie of it. He never bragged up a real thing when he finally had a good reason to."

"You're still bleeding," Tompkins says, reaching for Bean, touching more blood to his thumb.

"Mormon," Bean says, grinning, tossing an empty beer bottle into the creek where it bubbles and drops, settles into the silt. "Birr moved to Ontario, and a year outta high school I heard he'd died of a brain tumor. Everybody said he had it coming, that that's what lying fools get. That's what my mom said—'*That's what lying fools get.*'"

As the new blood dries Tompkins feels it tighten. He wants to taste it again, but Bean is watching, and he wraps his hand up in a fist, taps it softly on Bean's thigh.

"I thought Birr was okay," Bean says. "Liars don't deserve brain tumors. And shit, I really *did* used to steal baseball cards, but not at K-Mart. It was at Ford's downtown. I'd stuff 'em in my underwear, just like Birr said. He knew. He just put a spin on it."

"Shit," Tompkins says, looking high into the western sky at a slowly widening pattern of round white clouds, thinking now of the mornings this summer when he will wake before dawn after laying through short hours of shallow sleep.

These mornings Tompkins will wake thinking of Bean. He will wake hearing Thin Mikey's snore through the wall, and know that his mother is lying peacefully next to this man. These mornings Tompkins wants to sit beside Bean, like this now, hear Bean tell him one true thing, no matter if it's a lie. Something, anything, will do.

Tompkins will dress quickly in the pre-dawn, a purple light draping his room. Tompkins will lace and tie-up his boots, walk the block up to Fairview, point himself toward Bean's apartment, and begin the two miles. On the corner the 7-11 will be bright, empty but for the clerk, and one older man who drags a small white dog on a dirty leash. Tompkins will step into the 7-11's yellow light, becoming a part of the snap shot he thinks the truckers and cops can just make out as they speed Fairview. Tompkins pours himself a soda, pays, and sets off for Bean's.

These mornings traffic is spare, and walking he will regard the low hills to the east—a deep brown silhouette cast against a brightening ripe-plum sky. The traffic is one car, two—up, up, down—Fairview looking so long, so heavy and wide, as the taillights diminish and wink away, the boulevard rising then dropping toward downtown.

He will sit cross-legged on the sidewalk tilting his neck to see the Big Dipper, Mars, Cassiopeia, before he rises to walk past Tuxedo Inc. and The Fabric Depot, walk beyond Big Sir Waterbeds and Canned Food Outlet and Salvation Army, where furniture and bags of clothing lie mounded in the empty parking lot.

Soon he will be standing outside Bean's apartment, staring at the red diamonds painted on the black front door, wondering what he himself is doing, wondering why, and his heart rushes as he sits on the hood of Bean's car. He imagines Bean inside, tangled up with Sally Beecher, both deep in sleep, enfolded in the trance of skin on soft skin. There are never lights on, and Tompkins always hopes he can find it in him to try the front door, realize it is unlocked, then tip-toe into Bean's kitchen, his living room, his bedroom, crouch down, so close to Bean, listen to him draw and press breath, the same air Tompkins has breathed.

But, these mornings, Tompkins never checks the door, and he is ashamed of this fear, lost somehow within it. Yet now, sitting creek-side next to Bean in the heated summer 2pm, listening to him tell a new story, watching him smile through fast-coming swelling the Mormon has delivered, Tompkins thinks yes, tomorrow morning I will walk into Bean's, walk through the front door. Perhaps tomorrow morning, or the day after. Yes. Soon. I will check the door and it will be open. I will walk in and find Bean, sit beside him, and Bean will not wake. He will not wake, and I will take Bean's hand hanging low above the carpet, and I will hold it close, smell on it the turn of Sally Beecher's hip and her inside, smell the blackening fight scabs and the speeding red blood beneath. I will trace the veins on the back of Bean's hand, and they will point me places that one day I might go.

Creek-side, looking pleased and fearless, Bean says, "Let's just sit here a while. Fuck this day."

"Sure," Tompkins says. And he thinks, yes, Bean, let's sit. Yes, Bean, I will see you one morning soon, well before work, well before that Fairview fills up with its hot murmur, well before we really know what new fight lies before us.

WHERE HE'S LIVING NOW

I'm sitting window seat 14A, over the wing, so I can't see as much of downtown San Diego as I'd hoped. We're dropping into the city, the 727 lurching and shuddering for no reason I can figure. The weather is perfect springtime, and I can see this much: Golden light slapping to life the graceful stucco buildings of a hilltop park, the brown canyons and bunches of deep green palm and eucalyptus trees, a shaped blue bay and its patchwork sails, the docked stone-gray battleships and aircraft carriers. I've never been to San Diego, but my father lives here now and has invited me down. From this angle I have to say it looks pretty good.

The plane dips, and my stomach rolls. The plane rises, and my head, well, it hurts like shit. The boys had me up late last night, after our shift at the bar. The 8am flight out of Seattle did not come easily. But, that's the way of things. I haven't seen Dad in a year, not since he semi-retired, sold the house in Ballard, and bought a condo on a golf course somewhere down there. Plus, I'm feeling good about the fact I might see Gina, an ex of mine, while I'm in San Diego—she's supposed to be living with her mother near Del Mar, or La Jolla, or somewhere like that, where I can imagine the lean dark shape of her sitting beneath this Southern California sky drinking a glass of white wine, watching waves gather and press into a clean sandy shore. And I can imagine her mother—calm and confident, tall and hazel-eyed, pretty beneath years, looking like her daughter will—standing over Gina who takes her mother's hand and kisses it. A tender scene. The plane engines whine, and the woman sitting beside me gasps as we slow, and lower further down.

My own mother died five years ago this month, June 19. She drowned in the Payette River. In Idaho, rafting with a tour group. What a thing. Mothers aren't supposed to drown. Mothers aren't supposed to just die when their son is twenty-five, when their daughter is twenty-three.

This is what always leaps to me, and what is leaping to me now: The crowded mess of water wrapping my mother; the collapsing; the hard charge of throaty noise; the snap-turn of violence, then peace. There's no logic to it, and there never will be.

I'm straining to see Mexico through the scratched-up double-paned glass, the plane angling hard, scooting fast over the dry grid of a downtown looking dirtier the closer we get. Through my thin reflection—tired blue eyes, shaggy brown hair, pale cheeks in the windows—Mexico appears a murky dusk out there to my left, hazy mounded hills rising green through yellow air. I've never been to Mexico either, and I want to see it, but it fades as we lower, frustrating me as the ground rises and the tires shriek and the pilot hits the brakes.

"Did you see Mexico?" I ask the lady sitting next to me.

"Today?" She looks at my neck and the vine-work tattoos creeping above the collar of my shirt.

"Yes," I say as the plane slows. The click-clack of seatbelts unlatching fills the cabin.

"No," she says, standing with the others.

I've always gotten on with my father in a semi-strained manner. Fathers and sons. He's expected me to bring him pride and comfort, like any father would, and I, like any son, can't know if I have. In high school, Dad would take me to lunch downtown some weekends, or to Northgate Mall where we watched crowds of shoppers. He would get me a soda and a sandwich, and we would sit on the periphery. "That man there," he would say, pointing maybe to a clean-cut, strident man, "he's someone you should want to be like. You end up looking like him, you'll have few troubles."

"What could you possibly know about that guy?"

"A lot," he would say. "You look at things; you know things." Then he'd find a man with a ponytail, or a beer gut, or a seeming ambiguity, and he'd point again. "That guy lives a miserable life, son. Probably beats his wife, or never got himself one."

"Come on, Dad." I'd turn away, wishing I could be that man he was pointing at, so I could know, with certainty, how to refute my father's words.

"Aspire for more than that, Nick. Please," he'd say, and I'd hope to somehow fail in my father's eyes.

These conflicts have shifted, but remained, since Mom died, since I quit my law clerking job and started tending bar at Ernie Steele's—a dark, riotous place—and since I started with the tattoos in earnest. My dad doesn't understand what the ink-patterns could mean to me, why anyone would choose to mar the skin God gave them, though sometimes he pretends. He's asked me about the chain-link or the green tiger up my arm, about the walrus and the oysters and the *Alice in Wonderland* poetry across my back, and he's silently nodded when I've answered. Mom would get it, she'd know things about the itch and mystery of slipping images into your skin. My mother didn't turn away from much. I'm more like that now, and Dad, he's always been one to look straight ahead, no matter.

My sister, Lorrie, was here over the holidays, and says Dad's changed some, taken off the blinders of work work work, of thinking he has to go into the office eighty hours a week to finally, completely, become something more than the kind, if unsophisticated, lower-middle class man he was when Mom met him at Seattle Central. My sister says Dad's toned-down talking about one day letting loose, and started taking on life as someone truly interested in living it. My thought: We'll see.

I begin looking for Gina immediately amongst the bright drama of the terminal—the cloistered greeting parties, the bank of CNN televisions, the high-arcing ceiling, the potted palm trees, the tote-pulling flight attendants. This is stupid, I know. Gina won't be here. I haven't spoken with Gina in two months, not since the morning I drove her to SeaTac so she could fly back to San Diego, live with her mother for a while. That was a warm morning, and I held her hand. We listened to hyper morning radio. It didn't seem we needed to say one word, that there was any right way to put things.

At the gate she asked me not to call her, to respect her situation with David, the husband, that she was leaving him and me and all this for a while, and that she would call when the timing felt right. I haven't heard from her, which I understand, but do not enjoy. There was something—daring? corruption? certainty?—that's kept Gina in a near corner of my mind. I can't help thinking about the times we had sneaking around on David, driving up to First Hill and Georgetown bars afternoons when it was pissing rain and gloomy except for the laughter and the drinking. We would be back at my place on 15th and done by the time I had to go on shift, by the time Gina had to think about what was for dinner, by the time David was done putting contracts together at his office.

I ease through the crowd, my heavy carry-on slung over one shoulder, a clean yellow light draping all of us here. It would be something to see Gina—her long-legged grace and soft brown skin, her crooked bright smile and freckled shoulders. She's the house wife you always hoped existed, the one who would come into your bar with her husband and leave her number for you written in lipstick—*Gina: 494-9872 = Afternoons*. I mean really.

This is when I see my father, standing amidst the crowd, waving his hands above his head before he even sees me. Look at him—Panama hat, flip-flops, floral-print Hawaiian togs head to toe—he looks fresh off the tour bus. A whole new Maxwell Davis. I step toward him, wave a small wave, and then he's smiling wide, and this stirs a flutter in my belly. It's been a long time, and this is almost what I expected: My father waving, smiling, wearing something that makes people stare.

"Nick," he says, and steps forward to hug me.

"Dad." I lower my head, stepping into him, feeling his thick arms wrap me, smelling his sweet aftershave and the newness of his shirt.

"You look like Mr. Howell," I say, pulling away from him.

"Who?"

"Like a white Don Ho."

"Sure," he says, reaching to touch my arm, then my neck. "You look pale."

"I live in Seattle."

"We'll get you some of this sun." He winks at me. "And what the hell's all this crap on your arms?"

"Magic marker."

This is how my father and I have talked with each other for as long as I can remember. I thought our banter might go away, or evolve, or become something less relied upon, but habits don't like to step aside. It's a cool reliance, a comfort of discomfort that I've seen in men and wish I didn't own as I watch my father turn from me, heft my bag over his shoulder, and stride toward the baggage claim.

I've never spent three days alone with him, not since I was a boy. There was always my mother, or Lorrie. I watch him now, walking ahead of me. His calves are tanned. His sandals slap an unsteady rhythm against his heels. I glimpse our oblong reflection in a polished metal wall and think: No one would believe I am with this man, following him, wondering how I might come to know him now. I'm a little nervous. Three days seems like a long time.

I am thirty years old, I weigh 165 lbs., my name's Nick Davis, my sister lives in St. Louis, and my mother died five years ago. Did I say this? This is still so hard to admit, or to remember today, hard to hear myself think (she's dead?), as I'm certain it is for my father. Maybe that's what he's thinking right now in his lowered head as he weaves past flight attendants and Mexican families, a young woman being pushed along in a wheelchair, and a maintenance man sweeping invisible garbage into his dust pan—*Son, you look something like her* (she's dead?) *I can't even look at you.*

"Is my thirty-year-old son a college graduate?" Dad says as we stand, hands in pockets, watching bags circle on the carousel.

"Could be I am," I say, and my father's eyes light. I was enrolled in my final three classes when Mom died. I've been enrolled twice since then, including this past semester, but never have the heart to get past the syllabus day.

"No shit," he says, and I think about lying to him. How would he know?

I set a hand on his back, lower my head and kick one shoe against the other. "Nah," I say. I can feel him breathe out a long breath. "Some time soon."

—

It may be that Dad's changed since Mom died. It's a hard fact to determine, but he's gotten himself together. Who knows how a person will react to a loss like ours? Lorrie says Dad's slowed the drinking some, shifted his disposition, taken up golf again. He has lost some weight, and the kindness, the ease, of my mother seems to have come into him, but it's hard for me to recognize him as this.

My mother told me once why she'd get tired of my dad. "He's so determined to impress," she said, "and to *make* it. I mean Jesus, that's only one thing, Nick."

I thought I knew what she meant. I think I must have been twenty-one, twenty-two.

"Who the hell knows about marriage?" she said. "Grandeur and dearth." She had taken the afternoon off from her University of Washington research job—archeology—and met me downtown on my lunch break to eat turkey and cranberry sandwiches at a place called the Cyclops I.

It doesn't seem right, but I think Mom would have liked Dad better as what he's turned into. I think my father knows this, too, and the irony makes me a little angry, but he's the one living with what could have been.

He drives a Cadillac El Dorado now, a car he has always wanted, but was never able to afford. It's plum-colored with bits of winking chrome attached to it, and he's driving fast up the interstate.

"See those planes?" my father says, leaning toward the steering wheel, looking up and into the still blue sky. "Fly boys."

Three jet fighters—thin gray shapes—are flying low in a tight formation above the freeway to the north. "You might want to watch the road."

"The Miramar base is up ahead," he says. "Used to be Air Force, now it's Marines."

"Where they filmed *Top Gun*," I say. The planes tilt, show the underside of their wings in unison, and rise out of our vision as three small triangles.

"That's right." My father points silently at a huge green helicopter coming into view above the boxy plain apartments and a Barona Casino billboard to our left.

"Highway to the danger zone." I smile, and my father tries to watch the helicopter in his side-view mirror, in this moment not hearing or seeing me.

"There's a military presence down here," he says quietly. "Don't know how to feel about that." He looks at me and flinches, as if suddenly remembering I am here with him in his new Cadillac. "You at that bar still?" He slaps my knee. "Are you gonna get off that train anytime soon?"

"Let's not," I say holding my hand up. "Let's not travel there."

My father shakes his head yes, sure. I can feel he wants to say more, that he's fighting urges and words that would cast us into a place we've been a lot of times. "Smooth ride," he says, tapping the dash. "It's like driving your couch around."

"I've never considered driving my couch." The landscape here is tan, and deep green, dry and lush all at once. I watch the eucalyptus and oak trees standing beside mini-malls and bright billboards slipping by, and I wonder if Gina lives near this piece of the world. She could be just over that western rise, sitting down to read a book on the shaded back patio of her mother's house, crossing her tan legs, thinking about the times we had.

"Maybe you ought to," he says, and I don't know what this means. "Hungry?" He reaches over to rub my belly. I grab his hand, and it feels cold.

He takes me to a café in La Jolla, where we're seated outside under a striped umbrella. I can barely hear the waves slap into the beach as Dad orders for us both: "My boy and I will have the club sandwich, one each, and French fries." He nods at me. I shrug. The waitress writes our order, and I watch her walk away, the sway of her hips reeling Gina again to the front of my mind.

"Padres," my father says. "Tonight, against the Red Sox. Inter-league play." I watch him say this, his eyes widening, brightening. He's excited, and I wonder because of this look, if he's ever had anything with a married woman, or if my mother went down that road.

"Sure."

"Good seats," he says.

A slow wind shifts the air. The ocean smells briny, heavier and sweeter somehow than Seattle. I look up into the thinning midday overcast, spots of blue showing through. I never thought I'd draw a woman into having an affair, never really considered something like Gina, but like a lot of things, it played out despite what I thought. Gina started coming into the bar, at first with her hus-

WHERE HE'S LIVING NOW

band, then just with friends, then once or twice all alone, making the right eyes, saying the right things, and the momentum began. One afternoon I called the number.

"Pretty place," I say, nodding in the direction of the cliffs and the water.

My father takes in a full breath through his nose. "Love it. Can't get enough of it."

I think about asking him how he really likes it here, if he has many new friends, how he's living his life in a new city without Mom, or Lorrie, or me. But, the waitress is at our side lowering plates onto our table, and then my father is gripping his sandwich, taking big toothy bites. I open the catsup bottle and try to shake some out.

My first tattoo was my mother's maiden name—Virginia Reese Benedict—running along the white-skin underside of my left forearm. It hurt like shit, and I wanted it to. I got the work done two months after that morning my father called at 6am and told me all about her bouncing out of the raft and tumbling through the high water to get wedged beneath a rock.

"She's dead?" I said.

"Son," my father said, and he was crying hard. I shook deeply and dropped the telephone. I watched a city bus lurch and stop below my window. Someone had spray-painted "Cretins Fuck" in red on the roof.

The ink script of her name is bright blue and black, and it holds elegant and strong. I was scared at first to feel something so permanent come into me, but once it was there I was so glad, and

I am. It was shocking—the eking blood, the gathering contrast of those letters, the fact my mother was somehow cast anew, her birth name in her son.

My father's condominium is on the seventeenth fairway of the Canyon Ridge semi-private golf course. He tells me this, and that he's become a member here, as we roll up to the gate outside his neighborhood and he pokes his security code into the keypad.

"The code's your mother's birthday," he says, looking straight ahead at the gate as it lurches, slides open. My father watches this movement with a quiet pride that makes me sad. It's a low gate without sharp edges or points, and it doesn't seem it could stop anyone who was remotely serious about getting in.

The neighborhood is a mix of full-sized homes and town-house-style condominiums all stucco and painted various shades of brown. The streets slope up and down gentle rises where short palm trees and ferns stand next to square, bright-green lawns.

"This is it, the spankin' new neighborhood," he says as we round one corner. "Check out those jacarandas. They just plant-ed them."

"Not bad."

"Nice people here. Good neighbors. We're going to play golf with Jack Mandel tomorrow. He's letting you borrow his old set of irons. Calloway, though, nice clubs. Jack lives next door with his son. Nice guys, but his son, he has MS."

"Oh," I say, trying to picture just what my father's friend's son might look like. "That's not good."

"I think your mother would have liked it here alright."

I nod as he pulls into the driveway of his unit.

"Home sweet home," he says.

The neighborhood I grew up in, and the house my father lived in before he moved here, is at the absolute other end of this place he's living now. We lived in a modest 1920's-built home in the Ballard neighborhood of Seattle, a blue-collar Scandinavian fisherman-type of neighborhood. Walking into my father's new condo I remember the old house—three bedrooms, mine in the basement, the warm comforts of a fire my mother kept stoked through wintertime, the small wooden-fenced yard where our cat Clancy would sit and watch my mother garden.

My father's new place has high ceilings and southwest or Mexican-themed décor, if there's a difference—potted cacti, abstract pastel desert prints, curtains with little geckos stamped across them.

"Wow," I say, as he walks me through the kitchen, the hallway, into the den. Everything seems certain of what it is and where it should be. It makes me feel numb, out of place.

"You can sleep in here," he says, pointing into the den. "Or out on the living room couch. I know you're prone to couches."

"Where did all this come from?"

"Decorator," my father says. "When you buy the condo a specialized interior decorator is provided. Watch this."

We step into his master bedroom, he flips on the overhead light, and presses two little buttons on his painted-white bedside table. I hear the hum of a tiny engine. At first I think the bed is vibrating, and I'm thinking no way, but then I see a 30-plus inch television descend from the ceiling, and the curtains open to expose a tiny lanai and the pleasant green expanse of the seventeenth hole.

"Jesus," I say.

"Yep. Unpack your bags. Make yourself at home. Game's not for a time yet."

Sometimes I think Mom would have been all for me and Gina, if she could have gotten past the married part, seen us together, known how it was.

Gina was carnal with me, more than any girlfriend I've ever had, more than any one-night throw, and though this is an awkward thought, I believe my mother was a carnal woman. Gina has eyes that see more than the surface of things. She can look at you, know where you've come from, what you're wanting now, and how she fits into the puzzle of you. My mother had eyes like that, and I saw her turn them on men in a crowded room, or in traffic, or in a movie theatre. She would turn them on my father too, some nights after dinner and a second glass of wine. I didn't recognize any of this until after mother died, until after I got into it with Gina.

Before the Padres game, while my father is singing in the shower, I look Gina's number up in the local book. Her mother's name is Margarita Lorenz, and there are three listed. I call all three and get answers. I ask if Gina is in, and at the third number I am told yes, one moment. My chest tightens, my palms sweat. I take the phone out the front door and sit on the condo's front steps.

"Hello," Gina says in a sonorous manner that I absolutely recognize.

"Gina."

"Who's this?"

"Nick," I say. "Nick Davis . . . from Seattle, Ernie Steele's."

"Nick," she says. "What are you doing?"

"I'm in your city."

"How'd you know I was at this number?"

"Ingenuity."

There is a solemn quiet on the line that I didn't expect. I don't know what I expected exactly, maybe that she would say: Let's meet; come see where I'm living; it's so over with David; I know the best bar over in Del Mar, and there's this motel down the block . . .

"So," Gina says. "How's life?"

I tell her about the bar, about Seattle, about how I'm here to see my dad for a couple of days, about the same ol', same ol'. "I've thought about you plenty," I say. "I got some new work done— colored up the scene on my back yellow and blue."

"Yeah? I like that piece, but . . . it's, I'm, a lot more sane down here."

I sit, facing east, and the lowering sun is opening up the colors of the hills—the trees look purple, and the yellow grass is orange. In the distance, interstate traffic hums and snakes between rounded hills. Behind me, through the open door, my father is singing an old show tune within the hush of shower water.

"Can I see you maybe?"

"I guess," she says. "Maybe . . . yeah."

I wave to a mother and daughter who are walking matching beagles down the sidewalk. The little girl waves back, and the mother nods.

I ask: "What are you doing tonight?"

"Tomorrow's better."

"Tomorrow."

"Yeah, you know. David's actually here this afternoon, visiting, leaving tonight."

"That's timing."

"It's funny," she says, and clears her throat. "It might not be the very best time."

She tells me about David in the other room talking to her mother, about her job at a museum in Balboa Park, about how things have really fallen into place. She says she's not drinking much, if any, these days. I'm thinking, Je-sus, but I just tell her it all sounds great, right on, until she says she'd better go, that she'd better get off the line.

"So," I say. "Maybe tomorrow."

"You can call me." And she hangs up.

Walking into the stadium my father stops at a vendor, orders us fish tacos, asks me if I want a soda.

"What about hotdogs?" I say. "What about beer?"

"You get what you need," he says, paying. "These are delicious." He hands me the tacos, and we go to find our seats.

The stadium is three-quarters full. The Padres are no good this year, but the local Red Sox fans are out in force. Our seats are down the first base line, twenty rows up.

"This is living, son," my father says. "Feel the temperature. Look at the sky. This beats the hell out of the Kingdome."

"This is nice," I say. I haven't been to a ballgame in seven, eight years maybe. I look up, around. The crowd is milling and murmuring, and I like the energy of it all, the motion and the openness.

Our family would go to the old Mariners games. Lorrie hated it, always complained that it was too cold, that the Mariners sucked. She was young, eleven or twelve, and my parents pretty much ignored her even though she was right on the money. Mom and Dad liked the games. They'd drink beer, and my Mom would ride the umpires.

"Listen, son," my dad says. "I'm glad you came down here. It's been too long."

I nod, watching a high foul ball arc over the backstop. "It has been."

"Golf tomorrow," he says. "Maybe the Wild Animal Park the day after?"

"Sounds good."

After the fourth inning I tell Dad I'm going to take a walk, and I head for the corridor where I find a beer vendor and buy a pint. I walk through the open-air passageway drinking the acrid luke-warm beer, watching the bustle of families, teenagers on dates, clutches of shouting Boston fans, and cute young girls who all remind me of Gina in one way or another. I drink the beer quickly, buy another, and climb up the corkscrew ramp to the third level of the stadium.

From up here all this looks like a toy. The field is so green, the empty seats are so blue, the players and their uniforms are absolutely clean, perfect. I make my way to upper-upper left field where no one else is sitting. The announcer's hollow voice echoes through the stadium, and finds me. The sharp smack of the ball hitting the wooden bat. The clap and roar of the crowd sounds like a fast river. I fold down seat X25, take a full drink of beer, try to find my father in the distant crowd. He's out there, but I can't quite pick him out. I think, well, Gina could be out there, too, with David. I pan the stadium wondering how many of these people might have dabbled in infidelity, how many of them want things I've had, how many don't, and never will.

Down the row a security guard is walking toward me. We look at each other, "Section's closed, sir," he says.

"Why's that?"

"It's just the way they have it arranged," he says, and I can't argue with that.

Back in the seat next to my father I order another beer, and one for him.

"Take a walk?" he says.

"Just looked around."

"I could see you up there," he says, pointing. "Way up top. I knew that was you. They keep those sections closed for one reason or another."

"You could see me?"

"I know what you look like."

My father eyes me steadily, nods. He seems to want to etch this ordinary moment into his brain. I turn, watch the Padres jog out to their positions.

"The King of Beers," he says, holding his wax-paper cup to mine.

"You said it." I toast him, and we go back to watching the Padres lose seven to four.

My father hit me one time—punched me on the shoulder and shoved me to the ground. We were on a ski vacation with neighbors. It was evening and the adults had been drinking some. I was eleven. My sister told him I'd been hitting her, which wasn't true at all. I don't know why she said this.

"Hit the floor, champ," he said as he stepped up and gave it to me. "Not your sister." He smiled at this, and I couldn't say a word. I just shook, then ran out the front door of the cabin we'd rented, out into the blue evening light where it was snowing. I walked up the road for what seemed like forever, and when I finally turned around and came back to the cabin, my mother hugged me.

"You must've walked five miles," she said. "That takes some strength."

He's apologized a lot of times, and I've told him I don't hold it against him, but when I get to remembering it, how it felt to find myself on the cool tile floor, absolutely without the ability to stop my father from coming at me, I get a pinched feeling in my gut and I feel angry, feel like it would be easy to turn away from him for good. One time. A slip-up. But I can't lose it, I can only hide it.

My father punching me is what I thought of the morning he told me about Mom. I could taste blood in my throat, on my tongue. There was a stammer to my thoughts. I was afraid of him, and so angry. I wished he were standing in front of me, above the wrinkled dirty clothes and the empty bent beer cans in my studio apartment. I wished I had a bat, or a crowbar to hit my father with then. I wished I had his neck-flesh in my grip. And I was only partly sorry that I was wanting this.

My father steers us up the interstate fifteen miles in the Caddie, and back at his condo he says he's bushed, sets me up with linens and blankets. I tell him thanks again for the game, and he says again, "It's been too long, huh Nick? Golf here at Canyon Ridge in the morning." He phantom-swings. "Seven iron to a tight pin. You'll like this course." He feigns a putt, and goes off to bed.

I sit on the living room couch in the still yellow light. I think to turn on the television, but can't find the remote, so I remain there listening to the droning of the refrigerator. It is a quieter silence, one that fills this air, making me feel anxious and alone. I stand, see my reflection in the tall sliding-glass door, and for a moment am startled because I don't recognize myself in this scene.

I want to go out, get to a bar or a club where I can sit amongst people for a while. In the fridge I find a can of beer, snap it open and take a long drink. I find a sweater in my bag, slip it on, and it smells sweet and heavy with smoke from the nights I've worn it to work. I walk to my father's door, stand in the dark hallway listening for his deep and steady breath. Opening his door I feel like I did years ago, as a teenager, tiptoeing into his room, finding the keys on the dresser, back-stepping all the way into the living room. If I'd asked, he likely would have let me take the Caddie out, but this is another way we have been. Keeping secrets has always seemed like the right thing.

In the garage I disengage the automatic door, opening it stealthily by hand. The Cadillac starts quietly, hums smoothly. I back out into the hushed neighborhood street. There is no movement, only the press of golden streetlamp light. I put it in drive, and go.

The streets here are wider than home, and traffic is still heavy now, just past eleven. The dash lights are soft. The radio is playing the jazz my father likes, and I'm reminded in a quick moment of him taking me to school on his way to the office. I didn't like to talk much those mornings. I was always tired, and I remember it being constantly dark and wet, but he would ask me questions—What are you learning? How do you like your teacher? Isn't it funny how it rains so much here?

I roll past a darkened shopping mall and the red neon of the chain restaurants abutting the interstate. There's no neighborhood here, and everything seems too big, too broad. I circle the mall, follow the signs to an on-ramp, and turn south. I can get somewhere downtown for two drinks before last call.

I speed the five-lane—85, 90 mph—keeping pace. The Cadillac, it floats, seems to know this stretch of roadway by heart, and soon the downtown buildings show themselves. I take the City Center exit heading west, and at 11:40 I street-park and walk into a small bar called The Plus-One. Guitar music fills the long, narrow room. A pretty blonde woman hollers and whistles near the back corner pool table, says: "Pay up, motherfucker." The man she's talking to smiles, and walks through the dim red light toward me as I sit at the bar.

"Damn woman beat my ass again," he says, ordering a pitcher. "Don't ever think a woman can't beat you at a simple game."

I shake my head, and he walks away. It hasn't been twenty-four hours since I walked out of Ernie's, but it feels good to be out again, to be in a place with a jukebox and a pulse. I consider calling Gina. Maybe she knows the Plus-One, and would come down for a drink and some of the old talk. Her voice plays in my head—whispering the phone number, saying my name.

I order a draft, take a drink, look around. I'm the only one at the bar. The music shuts off and the couple at the pool table quit playing and simply stand, leaning shoulder-to-shoulder into one another. There is a round silence charging this space, too. I wonder if my father ever gets to this part of the city. I doubt it, and I wonder what I'm doing here. Dad's gonna wake me up at seven for golf. Shouldn't that be enough?

After my mother died, and I took the job at the bar, my father would come in some nights, sit up front and drink draft Rainier. He would watch me work, and ask me questions when it was slow. He never drank more than three pints, maybe four if he stayed a while. I don't think he understood what he was doing there. He probably wanted to be near me, to take a look at what I was.

"So, how often you have to change the kegs?" he'd ask.

"Depends on traffic." I'd look over his head.

"How much does one of those things weigh?"

He'd stare too hard at a lot of the people who'd come in. Maxwell with his yellow hair. Sheryl with her face all pierced. Sometimes Sully the Puzzle Man, his face and head all blue and white and inked up, would come in, do shots of Rumplemintz, and I'd shake his jigsaw-tattooed hand when he was on his way out.

"You know that man?" my father would say.

"Why not."

"It's a different world, boy."

The jukebox starts up again, playing a sad country song. I drink a second beer and ask the bartender if I can use the house phone.

"Local?" he says, handing me a cordless.

"Yeah."

"Make it quick then."

I find Gina's number in my wallet, then dial and listen to it ring until the machine picks up. I hang up, redial, and it's ringing again. This time I get an answer.

"Hello?"

"Gina."

"David?"

"Nick," I say, walking toward the front door, sheltering the phone from the music.

"Where the hell?"

"I'm at someplace . . . The Plus-One it's called."

"Goddamn."

"You wanna come down for a drink?"

"Where's your father?"

"I borrowed his car. Had to get out of the house." The song cuts out, and I'm talking two notches too loud. "Come on out with me."

"Tomorrow."

"Tonight."

"Goodnight, Nick."

"I'm gone tomorrow night," I lie, wanting her here now. "Seattle-bound."

"Forget it then," Gina says, pausing. "Let's just call it done."

"But I'm here for two days."

"Exactly."

Gina hangs up, and I know she's right. Whatever it is she said, it's right, and I feel like an idiot standing with an empty pint in one hand, a dirty bar phone in the other, in a place I couldn't find on a map if I had to.

I go to sit in the Cadillac and watch a solitary man amble up the sidewalk and away from me. I roll down the windows, and the night air is warm. Up the interstate traffic is light. The pavement is the color of rain clouds. I turn the music off, and the wind hushes my anger, my embarrassment, my displacement. But in this it seems I could go, just drive and drive—east into the hills and then the desert, north through these clustered lights and unknown cities, then into L.A. and its choke of humanity. So many things, for a time, could be new again. My father wouldn't know how to find me, or where. What would he do in the morning? Where would he think I'd gone? Where would he look for me?

When my father's exit comes up I hesitate, but take it, feel I have to, then drive toward his house, punch my mother's birthday into the security keypad. I steer through his neighborhood, past the green garbage cans lined up at curbside. I quietly open his garage and pull in.

In his dark kitchen I stand at the sink and drink two glasses of water.

From behind me: "She drives pretty nice, doesn't she?"

I spin. "Holy shit, Dad."

"You could have just asked."

Some water catches in my throat, and I begin to cough. "Hell, I'm sorry. I don't know."

He looks at me as if he feels sorry, as if he knows how my talk with Gina went, like he recognizes a weakness, or a hurt, that he's had, too. "Grab me a beer."

"Fine."

"I'm not lecturing my thirty-year-old. It's almost two. I just want a beer."

"Let's have a beer then."

We sit across from each other—he on the sofa, me on the side chair. He doesn't turn a light on. The room is dull silver and gray with moon or city light.

"Toss me the keys, Nick," he says, and I do.

"It's a real nice car, Dad."

"Thanks," he says. "Maybe one day you could own one."

"I felt like a drive," I say. "I guess that was all."

He tilts the beer, takes three long swallows, then looks at the keys in his other hand. "Will you do me a favor?"

"I think I could."

"Come sit next to me," he says, patting the cushion beside him. "I want to see something. Father and son." He finishes his beer, and bends the can between his thumb and index finger.

I stand and go to sit next to him, figuring I can oblige him this. He smiles at me, and thanks me when I sit down. The shadows paint his creased face a deep blue. I drink from my beer.

"Could I see it?" he says, pointing to my arm.

My heart speeds up, and I look him in the eye. I know what he wants—yet, I never thought he knew, because he has never asked, never even mentioned it—and I pull my sweater sleeve up, reach my arm across his lap, show him her name. He doesn't speak, and neither do I. My father runs two fingers over the words, the skin. His hand is steady, soothing, and I am surprised because I am trembling. I remember Gina touching these ink lines softly, in this unsure manner. He nods and nods, affirming something wise in his mind, and maybe knowing something new. Then he stands, and he thanks me.

"Sleep," he says, winking, a kind and nervous gesture. "Be ready for some good golf. Tomorrow is already here."

I pull my sweater sleeve down. "I'll try to be." I look away, and hear him pad down the hallway and shut his door.

We're on the Canyon Ridge first tee by eight. It's a warm morning, the lawnmowers whining, the big sprinklers hissing, clacking. We're drinking coffee, Dad chit-chatting with his friend Jack Mandel. I want to say something about last night, but this doesn't seem the time. I'm wearing shorts and a polo-type shirt with geese and fisherman printed across it, something he had picked out for me, and Jack Mandel is looking at my bare arms and neck uncertainly.

"You know you can't out-drive me, Jack," Dad says. "Me, or my boy."

"You got that wrong," Jack says.

My father nods to me and I nod back as I turn away, yawning. My father tees it up, then I do, then Jack Mandel rips one fifty yards past both of ours.

"I guess you got that wrong, Dad," I say as we walk off the tee, and he looks at me like I should shut the hell up, like I shouldn't embarrass him here.

He walks beside me, Jack Mandel just behind us. "You need to make a full turn, Nick. It's all timing, this game." And he nods to Jack.

"I don't really even play golf anymore."

"Still," he says. "Why not know what you're not doing."

We pace through the round. Jack Mandel remains mostly to himself, and I wonder what kind of friend he is to my father, what kind of people Dad has close to him now. On the eighth hole my father hooks his drive into the row of stucco houses lining the left side of the fairway. It whacks off a red-tiled roof, sounding like gunshot.

"Good Christ," my father says, and he tees up another ball.

Jack Mandel gives me a brief knowing look, and my father hooks another ball that whacks into a house precisely like his first. My father shakes his head. "I'll drop," he says, "up in the fairway. Save us all the misery."

I hit my drive and walk up the fairway, veering left toward

the netted fence-line that runs between the course and these still and silent homes, homes like my father's now. In their backyards are gas barbeques, green-cushioned lawn chairs, tall bulbous cacti. Some have gem-blue swimming pools. I look for my father's drives, but they're gone, ricocheted into a bush, or out into the empty neighborhood street, maybe into one of these pools. These look like lonely homes to me, sequestered and staid, and I wonder what our old home in Ballard, or my own apartment's front door, may have ever looked like to a stranger trying to piece together the life behind them. On a second-floor balcony I see a woman. It takes me a moment to recognize the human shape of her, sitting on a lawn chair in a white blouse and baby-blue pants. It makes me feel strange that she's been watching. She waves to me, silent, smiling, looking pretty from here, and I wave back.

The sky is nearly cloudless, thin wisps of white painted here, there. I watch a hawk float high above my father, who miss-hits another shot, says, "Shit, shit, shit," and marches toward his ball. Over my next shot I look back toward the woman on the balcony, who is standing now. She is thin, and taller. Sweat beads on my forehead. I think of Gina and last night, and get embarrassed all over again. I get mad at myself. I wish I could see her today, tell her I was a little desperate last night, a little lonely, or sentimental, that I *know* our time is over, but don't know why. I'd like to touch her hand once more, say, "Don't think of me as a mistake." I wish in this moment that I knew, now, that I won't call her today, that I won't ever want to see her again. But, I may want to, need to, and I wonder if this is fine, too.

When I get to the green and look back, the woman on the balcony is gone. "Perfect," I say.

"Not from this angle," my father says.

At the turn Dad buys me a Danish and another cup of coffee.

"Jack's beating the hell out of us," I say.

"I've got to work on my short game—Jesus, if I could make a five-footer I could play this game."

"That's what a lot of people think."

"You know Jack's boy," my father says quietly as we walk toward the tenth tee. "Great kid. Twenty-four. Probably has a year to live."

"Jesus," I say. "Just one?"

"He's a baseball fan like you wouldn't believe. Knows everything. Maybe after the round," my father says, taking the red fuzzy cover off of his driver, looking around for Jack Mandel, who is eating a hot dog and easing towards us. "Let's after the round go have you meet him."

"Next door?"

"He can really only move one finger. John's his name. He's at home with the nurse Jack's had to hire. What a circumstance."

Jack Mandel beats us both, and at the end of the round my father hands him twelve dollars, says, "That's the third time in three weeks you took my walkin' around money, Jack."

"I've got to walk around, too," Jack says, and I'm thinking this sounds weird, or wrong, considering his son. But, I suppose he's well over that kind of thing.

As we drive the half-mile back to the condo, past Mexican men wearing pith helmets and trimming the tight, small lawns, my father tells me I played okay, that I should be out on the course more often.

"If I had your natural talent," he says. "Senior tour, son." He flexes his bicep and growls.

"Don't hurt yourself."

"You know his wife left him. Last year."

"Who?"

"Jack. She said that John, that their whole dynamic, was too much." He pulls into the driveway, shifts it into park. "Can you believe that shit?"

"I guess we've had worse," I say, looking over at him. He rubs his neck slowly, looks out his side window toward next door where Jack Mandel is just pulling up in his Lincoln.

"I guess you're right."

Inside I pour myself a glass of milk, tell my father I'm going to lie down for a few. He says fine, you're on vacation, but don't go down for too long.

My mother is buried in Yakima, the town she grew up in. Her headstone rises from the crest of a little knoll with a walnut and two oak trees planted nearby. It's where her family plot is, a real pretty place. About once a month I drive the two hours up and over Snoqualmie Pass, past Cle Elum and Ellensburg, through all that open land on the other side of the Cascades and into Yakima. I bring flowers and some shears so I can keep the place looking right. It's not as hard as it might sound, or as sad as it sometimes seems it should be. Kneeling in the tight grass I'm able to breathe like I should, able to know one place with certainty, even if it's just a few square feet, and by the time I drive home I'm hardly able to remember how I came, or how I returned. There's a comfort in that.

When I wake on the couch I have a slow, dull headache, and I wonder for a moment where I am, how long I've slept, where my father is. I walk into the kitchen for a glass of water, and I see the note he's left me. *Next door playing Scrabble with the boys. Just come on over, let yourself in.* I pop three Tylenol, change and clean myself up a bit before I walk next door.

I knock twice and Jack Mandel answers, still dressed in his golf clothes. He's not wearing shoes, his graying hair is sticking up on top, and he looks about five times more relaxed, like he's had a beer or two.

"Nick," he says, extending his hand. "Get yourself in here."

I shake his hand. "You swing a nice club," he says.

"Thank you." He leads me into the living room. The layout of his place is precisely the same as my father's. The interior designer used a couple of different tricks here, bringing more vegetation into play—all kinds of potted plants that may or may not be real.

"The guys are out back. Soda? Beer?"

"Beer," I say. "Why not?"

He leads me into the kitchen. From here I can see out to the back patio where my father is speaking to a boyish and exceedingly thin man in a bulky wheelchair who must be John. Begonias and miniature palm trees wrap around the patio's concrete slab, two tall eucalyptus trees stand above, and beyond them is the golf course.

A Scrabble board sits on the glass-top table next to John and my father. John has blond hair, almost white, and wears wire-rimmed glasses. My father is waving his arms and laughing.

"You're still in Seattle?" Jack hands me a cold can of Miller.

"Yeah," I say. "Seattle."

"I couldn't take that weather. No sir, not anymore. We lived on Mercer Island." He snaps open a can of beer for himself. "Heard you're going to the Wild Animal Park tomorrow. Nice place. African *and* Asian elephants."

I follow him to the glass door and onto the patio.

"Nick," my father says. "I thought you went Rumple Stiltskin on us." He laughs loudly, raises his beer into the air, and looks at John who strains a smile. Jack Mandel laughs with my father.

"This is my son, John," Jack Mandel says. I look to John, who lifts his index finger, blinks, says "Hi" in a low, wet tone.

"Hey," I say.

"Have a seat," Jack Mandel says. "You can get in next game."

"John'll probably embarrass you," my father says. "I don't think I've beat him since last month."

"You got me the day before yesterday," John says. His voice quavers, and he breathes in a little saliva.

"Right. Right."

John is the thinnest person I've ever seen. He can't weigh eighty pounds. He steers his wheelchair toward me. It lurches, stops.

"You're from Seattle?" he asks, using the same cadence and inflection as his father. "Isn't it like the tattoo capital of the world? And isn't that like, so five years ago?" He winks at me, and I realize he's giving me shit. I don't know how to feel about this.

"That all could be true." I drink a mouthful of beer.

"Nick's got a thing for the ink," my father says, pointing at his own forearm, rubbing his skin as he did mine last night, and I'm thinking: What is going on here? I'm wondering where my father got a hold of a phrase like that. He has a mischievous look on his face, a look like I haven't seen in god knows. His eyes shoot from Jack Mandel's to John's to mine, and I wonder what all my father's shared with them about the history of himself, of me, of Lorrie, of my mother. This is a place my father is at ease, and I feel his comfort creep into me, too.

"Yeah, what's with all this?" Jack Mandel says, pointing toward my forearms.

"All important stuff," my dad says.

I shrug, shake my head. "Let's just stick to Scrabble."

"Fresh game?" John says, adjusting his chair back toward my father.

"Fresh game," my father says.

"The Mariners have been in the tank since the middle of May," John says.

"No shit," my father says.

Jack Mandel reaches across the table, begins tossing the lettered game tiles into the little cloth bag. The big eucalyptus trees shift as a warm breeze presses. I look up and watch a leaf loosen itself and spin toward the table.

"You remember how to play this game?" my father says. "You have to know something about words, and something about gamesmanship."

Someone out on the golf course yells "Fore!" as the twirling, falling leaf lands on John's head. John doesn't notice it. My father reaches over and gently lifts it off, tosses it over his own shoulder like it's going to give him good luck.

"You're gonna wish I *didn't* know," I say.

"Oooh," John says.

"The man wants to play," Jack Mandel says. "Max, you raised a gamer. Choose a tile. Closest to A goes first."

"If you get confused, Nick," Dad says, twirling his index finger around his right ear, opening his eyes wide. "Jack, or me, or John over there might be kind enough to help you out."

I look at him straight and serious, and for a slow moment he holds my stare. My father. I love him. And I am so glad I am here, across this table, three feet from him, and closer than I have been in years. He winks at me, and his friend Jack presses out a high nervous laugh, a gesture that tells me he too knows just what we're doing in this place, all of us.

"Good luck to you, son," my father says. "This is not as easy as it might look." He reaches toward me, holding out the small maroon bag.

"You're *all* going to need the luck," John says, darting his eyes toward Jack who clears his throat, and rubs his hands together over the board.

"Thanks, Dad," I say, winking back at him. I take a long swallow of beer, and close my eyes to reach in and choose my letter. "I'll keep that in mind."

NORTH

We sped the two-lane into Canada, morning washing the rearview orange, Colin beneath the backseat afghan, already gone.

You touched my waist, asking, "Who else knows?"

I couldn't answer.

Spring clouds loomed as giants.

Midday, we were on his porch, unfolding the body. I didn't know his wife, so I let you explain. She knelt. Her yellow hair, her blushing skin, his empty form, all permanent as I stepped away to watch birdless trees flutter and sway.

DENTISTS

They find another dentist floating in the canal, and Avery worries. The news: This is the fifth in two weeks—dentists, blindfolded and tethered and buoying in the aqueduct that slips by the backside of Avery's home. He lives alone, and is thirty-one years old. The wife is gone. She moved out, packing his television with her, more than one year ago. He has not replaced the television.

This morning Avery pads out the front door in pale bare feet to retrieve the paper. A solitary joy. So much strange bad news—black men denied breakfast, forty-pound house cats, singing politicians—and now murdered dentists, all from this city, all dumped in the canal that casts a charming hush through Avery's bedroom window in all seasons. The canal eases water from the lake to the reservoir, passing just beyond the low wooden fence in Avery's backyard. The canal has a cement bed and red gravel banks, and he has planted begonias beside the twelve-foot swath of water.

Avery shakes his head as he eats toast, reads on, drinks his coffee. The craziest of worlds. Never predictable. Avery cashiers at the new Market Grocery, and uses current affairs like a salve, making his time at the register a pleasant action. The dentists are what everyone has been talking about, his number one conversation starter, his sound bite. He stresses his personal proximity to the canal as he rings-up toilet paper, canned peaches, apples, corn chips. Worry creeps into each inflection—"Imagine, gagged and blindfolded, dead before they hit the water." People gasp, contort their expressions, say, "My god, watch yourself." Avery says, "I don't pull teeth," and pauses, strangely elated by their fear, "but still—it's unsettling." And they nod.

His is a pleasant, smaller city, warm now in the heart of spring, hopeful budding trees lining so many of the streets. Murders are uncommon here, almost unheard of. There is riff raff, but they are seldom seen. Avery's neighbors are kind, and worried like he that their homes along the canal have been exposed to some rumbling wrong, some unsavory movement. They have begun inviting Avery for coffee, or dessert, or evening cocktails, trying to enhance solidarity, and to discuss what the police and newspapers have reported about the murders—how they should stay in after dark, how they should report anomalous events, how they should check in on each other at least once a day. Avery has not yet taken up the offer, but enjoys the comfort of the gesture, feels a deferred security amidst the quiet pall draping the neighborhood.

Today Avery will work the ten to six, register sixteen, between Karen and Louisa. It's a stroke of luck; these are the two women he's had his eye on—cute, available, nicely built. Avery's wife left him, she said, because he was jealous, suspicious of every man she spoke with. She left him because he does not share her ambitions for designer clothing and furniture, for new cars and homes. She also believed he watched too much television news—the five local stations, CNBC, The Weather Channel, CNN—and she claimed that having Avery know the first and last names, and having Avery imitate the voice and mannerisms of each newsperson, was more than she could take. There is still a small love between them, a reluctance to divorce.

Avery's wife lives five blocks away in a complex of newer town-homes, but hasn't spoken with him since January 25th. He is sad for this, but feels it's her place to call him. He drives the Mercury by her apartment on the way to Market Grocery now, and Avery thinks of her nearly every time. This morning he remembers how her skin felt underwater when he would touch her in the bath, how it was tender and unreal, like rubber or hard-boiled eggs. But wonderful. Then he thinks of the dentists floating past his house in the deep night, their skin frigid and dying. Avery shivers, turns up the radio, wonders if his wife has been reading the papers and maybe thinking of his little house on the canal, the one she lived within for three years, two months, eleven days.

The customers at the new grocery love Avery. He is witty and friendly, younger and clean-shaven, always willing to disperse coupons and point out upcoming sales. He has watched young ladies switch into his longer line to have their groceries rung up by him. This makes him happy, gives him a shimmering pride, something management has noticed. Avery is the rumored upcoming employee of the month, something that only came to pass once in Avery's six years, eight days at his previous grocery job.

Karen and Louisa are both looking lovely today. They smile, say hello, and Avery answers with a, "Hello, gals. There was another murder."

"No," they say, softly biting a knuckle. "Another dentist?"

"It's in the paper," Avery says. "The fifth in two weeks. Read up on your break."

They say they will, Avery opens his register, and the day begins.

The grocery is busy, and Avery feels the rhythm of banter and checking enter him. It is smooth and steady, a submerged comfort, like breathing. Avery feels vibrant, awakened by the movement and murmur of the grocery. The florescent white light charges the air. His mind speeds, and he is able to think not only of the rung items, and the small talk, but of the pantries and the freezer shelves where these groceries will sit—spaghetti and broccoli, frozen waffles and sourdough bread. The Market Grocery is in a fine new neighborhood—gently curving streets lined neatly with familiar two-story homes and thin young trees. Avery pictures these homes with their clean, ordered kitchens, their stainless-steel cookware, their wine racks and fancy appliances. He smells the meals prepared, hears the television news from the eight-inch countertop TV. The newsman is talking about dentists, the dentists, a serial occurrence of murder— "It is a limited, vocation-oriented tragedy, but who is to say it will remain such." Avery wonders if maybe he has rung up one of the now-murdered, and it comes to him that he is due for a cleaning. It has been ten months, twenty days.

"Good morning," he begins his conversations as people step forward, unload their carts onto the lurching conveyor belt. "Crazy world out there."

"I know," the people say. "Murders, awful. Even if they were dentists."

"People are people," Avery says. "You know," and he pauses, looks them in the eye. "I live on the canal where they've been finding 'em."

"I've heard it's a cult thing, the murders," the people say.

"Have a pleasant day," Avery says. "Don't get a toothache." And there is an unsettling tremble in his belly. He thinks of his wife sitting in her apartment alone. She watches his television—a blue and silver window on the world—and eats popcorn, but it seems to Avery that she may not be safe, not in this city now.

Break time and Avery pours himself a tall cup of coffee. He goes to sit in the Mercury parked in the grocery's side lot and listens to the radio. He enjoys the privacy. He watches customers walk in and out. Among them—suddenly—is Avery's wife, walking into his store. Seeing her, his heart jumps—it has been three months, four days. He thinks again of her in the tub, her moist, pliable skin. She loves bath oils. Look at her. She is graceful and proud, her hair dyed black-black now, her stride still long and cunning. Avery thinks of the time she told him, "You being a grocery clerk, it embarrasses me."

"It's what I like to do," Avery says aloud now in the Mercury. These are the same words he thought to utter, but did not, when his wife spoke of her embarrassment. "Should I change what I like?" He drinks from his coffee. "No."

The DJ on the metal rock station makes a joke about the murdered dentists, something about bridgework and cavities, root canals. The joke, Avery thinks, is distasteful, and together with seeing his wife it makes him angry. He's known his wife for twelve years this month, and he wishes they would talk sometimes.

"You have my television," Avery says as his wife emerges from the store, her arms bear-hugging a full sack. He can see a head of romaine lettuce, and a bag of wheat pasta topping off the bag. He is still in the Mercury, and his wife does not see him, cannot hear him as she loads into her new Jeep. She has a good job. She has money. "You don't need my television," Avery says, and he watches his wife back out and steer the Jeep out of view.

The actions of the day fall out. People keep buying groceries; Avery keeps ringing them. Karen and Louisa read of the latest murder—he was a specialist, a widower with three children, found tangled in a grate further south than the others—and they express their shock. Avery tells them how he lives just upstream from the place where this dead man was hauled out, how this dentist may have floated through his yard in the small hours of the night.

"Like the others," they say. "You've told us about. God, be careful Avery. Please." He smiles again. They look away coyly.

His shift ends and Avery punches out, returns to the Mercury. To the west the evening sky is radiant, ineffable oranges, purples, reds. It's all darkening slowly, casting bubblegum light against his

Mercury. There is good hope in this light, Avery thinks, and the lingering menace of wrong news, of the murders, leaves him for a time. He stands beside the Mercury, looks west, runs his index finger over the round left headlight. A soft, black smudge. There is the gathering rumble of boulevard traffic as Avery settles into the Mercury, turns the key, pulls a heavy breath, and steers into the coming night.

Avery is just passing his wife's townhouse when he quickly slows and steers into her parking lot. The Mercury's headlights pan the bright-white gauze of the buildings. The clean, wide building stands four floors high. The trim is blue. It was built two years ago—220 units, a pool, a clubhouse—and Avery has heard it is nice. She lives in number forty-five, a ground-floor unit. He parks the Mercury and strides to find her.

The open-air hallway is so quiet. He wonders what he will say to her, if he will admit his worry, or his loneliness. Avery wonders if they might simply embrace and fall into a familiar peace. No one is around, not that Avery can see, and he hears no rustling, no footfall on the stairs, no movement seeping from inside his wife's apartment. He knows he has the right place. Avery has stood here once before, eighteen days after she left him, but that night he couldn't muster the will to knock, and after twelve minutes he walked away without his wife knowing he was ever there. There is so much we can do, Avery thinks, without the world's knowledge.

He knocks loudly three times. Waits. He knocks again, then tries the door. Locked. Avery walks the hallway to where the apartments face onto a courtyard. There is no one in the swimming pool, but there are six lighted apartments dotted here, there. He hears the crackling voices of televisions pitch down into the courtyard as he steps onto his wife's small back porch. There is a sliding glass door showing his dull, gray reflection. He knocks on the glass, and it rumbles like ten-mile thunder. No answer here, either. Avery tries the door, and it sucks open and slides, a seal broken. Something stands up inside of Avery—fear? compassion? worry? love? joy?—and he pushes aside the drawn curtain and steps into his wife's living room.

It is dark, and Avery stands dead still. The apartment smells like rosemary and new carpeting. He lets his eyes adjust, then finds a light switch and clicks it on. The first thing he sees is his television set propped neatly on a short table in the corner of the room, its glass reflecting his distended silhouette. There it is, he thinks, ah ha. Avery turns to see an open kitchen, a shallow dark hallway, three prints of black and white photographs hanging along the far wall. He makes for the hallway, feeling the rising urge to see her new bedroom and bathroom, the rooms where she undresses and eases herself into soft clear water. He has nearly forgotten where he is, yet wonders if other men have walked this hallway, eased into this bedroom, seen its order, smelled its sturdy comforts. He lights the bedroom and sees a dresser, a bed, a small picture frame on the nightstand. Who is in this frame? Avery moves to it, bends down, sees that it is him, smiling, giving the camera the thumbs up.

He sits on the bed and studies the photo. His wife took this picture at the beach, in Oregon, in wintertime. He is flexing his biceps, smiling wide sitting on a driftwood log. It was five years ago, when they had just begun to become more than long-time friends, when they had just begun to learn a sameness, a bright connection. Their marriage was seven months away. They had driven through the night to get there, through blue rain and green wind, over one mountain pass. They told stories. The one he remembers now is of his wife's high school cheerleading team traveling to Canada her senior year. One of the girls, now a nameless friend, went missing. Just vanished, his wife had said, gone. No one ever knew if she ran away, or if she was taken. The team stayed on two extra days, scouring the city in groups of three, four, then returned home, minus one. Avery remembers his wife leaping and laughing through a cheer routine on the dark, wet sand of that beach where he sat on a log and smiled and gave the camera the thumbs up. He is surprised to remember all of this.

Avery stands and smoothes the bed's blue covers. He returns to the living room, and suddenly the murdered dentists leap into his mind. What were the last things they saw? He looks at the backside of his wife's front door, and he is worried. He is worried for their city, worried for his wife who leaves her rear door unlocked, and who might bring men who are not him into this room where he now stands with a chilled sweat in his hands. Avery is worried about what next, about whether his wife will burst through the door and find him and hate him even more, about whether he will reconcile with her, or stop liking his job at the grocery, or finally reclaim his television. Can any of this find me? Here? The quiet of his wife's apartment rings broadly in his ears.

Avery lowers himself onto his knees. He presses his palms and fingers firmly into the low-cut beige carpet. Avery shuts his eyes, pushes at the floor, feeling his triceps and forearms ache generously. He thinks of the dentists. Has another been absorbed into his canal? Into the always-gone? Avery thinks of Karen and Louisa. What would they think of him here, on his knees, in this place he should not be? Breathing deeply, spots of turquoise and purple wash the dark behind Avery's eyes. Then, suddenly, Avery hears footsteps drum in the hallway—a shallow echo approaching. He holds the air tight in his lungs, keeps his eyes shut, hopes that these coming steps are, yes, his wife. He begins to smell her—the cloying honeysuckle air, the soap-clean skin—as the footsteps march, march to the doorway—pause—then fall away. Avery opens his eyes, and he is disappointed. These steps were not hers?

He stands, and below him, cast into the carpeting are his handprints. Avery steps backwards, then across the room, where he squints and cocks his head and sees with certainty this one place he has been. Within the matted footprints the mold is sharp and clear. His two hands reaching.

Silence shapes his wife's living room. He stands amidst it for a moment before he steps across the room, unplugs the television, pockets the remote. Avery cradles the set in his arms, and walks the awkward, heavy box out his wife's back door. In the still parking lot he sets it on the Mercury's passenger seat. The television sags and pinches the black vinyl. Avery shuts the door easily, quietly, and returns to his wife's apartment, finds a broom leaning in the fully-stocked kitchen pantry. In the dim living room light Avery sweeps away the maze of footprints, smoothes all the carpet around his handprints. He tiptoes and back-steps, excitement rising within him. Soon he is at her back door, the room is swept so nearly clean, the television table empty. Only the handprints remain. With the broom in one hand Avery slides shut the door, and makes for the Mercury. Let this be a leading mystery for his wife. Let her deduce that it was him, or be afraid it wasn't. Let her call him, and ask and maybe threaten to phone the police.

He drives home, fast and pleased, through the warm spring night, excited to set the television up on a table, click on the local news to get the latest, then maybe a game show, a sitcom. He hefts the television into his stilted, quiet house, and finds that a good place for it is the kitchen table. Avery unwraps a frozen pizza, and sets it in the oven. He locates a can of beer in the refrigerator, snaps it open, swallows the cold bitter liquid. The television is empty black. Plastic and glass. Avery wonders if maybe his wife is home now, standing above his handprints, trembling in a space she thought was private, her own. You can do nearly anything to a person in this world, Avery thinks, when you imagine it, open your mind to it. What are the things that stop you?

The local news—with a reporter Avery does not recognize— leads with the story of the murders. A suspect has been arrested, but he remains nameless. Photos of the victims, wet and bloodless, are cast upon the screen one at a time, and the newscaster is somber. The story ends and Avery decides he will have a cigarette, a lingering habit. He finds his pack in a kitchen drawer, steps into the backyard and lights up. The canal says: shhhhhhhh, shhhhhhhh. The television casts glints of blue and silver through the back window. His trees stand silent and catch the light. He walks to his low wooden fence, leans against it, and smokes. The canal slips by, its movement stealing sound. It is full dark now. There is no noise, or light, or movement from his neighbors, just he and this stretch of water. I could be the last one on earth, he thinks. Then what? But, the television light still pulses a frantic cadence—a vapid, comforting motion—and someone must be behind that light.

Avery pulls more smoke and gazes upstream into. The water emerges, emerges, and Avery sees humps in the water, dark and bobbing. He leans out over his low wooden fence—the water is hunched in places. His gut clenches. He cranes his neck, and the water-humps dip and disappear into the gloss. Avery envisions himself asleep these nights when the dentists have coasted into and through his backyard. Momentary and unseen. One. Two. Three. Four. Five. His heart is fast, and Avery squints to see through the cool, damp air. The water is smooth now—leaning, listing—and he tosses his cigarette butt in, hears it hiss, sees it press into the fabric and begin a transient ripple.

Avery lowers his head, crosses his arms, slowly closes and opens his eyes—listening, breathing, listening. So much nothing, nothing, until the telephone rings, echoing sharp and loud in his kitchen. A bright announcement drumming the night. And Avery turns, thinking now to run, wanting in this moment to reach through the skittering blue light, and answer.

THE CROSSES

I always had to help Ruby with the straps. Ruby was the neighbors' daughter, home from Eastern after flunking out third semester.

The black plastic squealed at her wrists, the bed-frame groaning as she shut her eyes whispering a name that wasn't mine into the flannel pillowcases.

When we started she'd bite my ear. When we finished she'd make us coffee cut with Jameson and sugar cubes.

It was the winter my wife drove her Honda into the wide glow of America one icy midday, and I never saw her again.

Ruby was red-headed, pixy-thin and so young, though her eyes said she was already pitted by life.

When Ruby heard about my wife, she started coming around. It didn't take long for what would happen to happen. And when she brought the straps out that first time it didn't surprise me.

—

In March my wife turned up in Las Cruces. A doctor with a southern accent phoned, said there'd been an accident. My wife was stable, though the man driving her car had died. She was badly shaken. She'd asked him to call on me.

This was a foggy Tuesday morning. I was running fingertips over the nesting-dolls tattooed across Ruby's feet. She smelled like lemonade, soap, warm vinyl.

Ruby and I took our time driving south to retrieve my wife—three or four days of blue highways and motels and using those straps.

By the time we got to that hospital all the nurse knew was my wife had walked out of there holding hands with two men.

I began to ask one thing, Ruby leaning warm against me.

The nurse simply turned her wide, happy face to us, saying, "Sweetheart, I can't tell you any more than that."

SOLSTICE

We let the city bus slip and hiss back into the night, deciding we could walk and wondering just what were we doing there.

It was late—3am, raining like a mother—and we were fully drunk. We'd been at the Comet Tavern, Ernie Steele's, then Beth's Café for pancakes and sausage. Then Jane was driving into a lamppost—somehow damaging none of us, only her old Dodge—and then we were making our way toward Max's rickety house up Greenwood where I was planning on getting in good with Janie before Max did.

It was so late. We were trodding through one of the dingy neighborhoods off Aurora Ave.—squat '70's homes lining the street, the hard rain drumming aluminum siding—and there she was. Split in two. A woman in the blood-pink dress, lying headless on the asphalt. She was Mexican or something. Her face looked dark and almost shocked, surprised, balancing upside-down—a lonely sideways headstand—on top of matted oil-black hair.

The body was strewn like raccoon garbage in the dark wash of the narrow street. We'd been looking down, bitching about that weather, then she was there, and there, dripping shadows, or blood. When we realized what was in front of us I pissed my pants a little, and Max puked his breakfast. Janie started running, silent and faster than anyone.

Looking at this woman wholly and completely undone, I was scared, and I was exhilarated. Every shape and smell cut clearly through the beer and vodka. Crystalline. Amazing. And I liked it, my life, just then.

Max was making noises like a dog, bent to his knees and palms on someone's spotty front lawn.

"Wow," I said. "Wow. Get the fuck up, Max."

"Is this real?"

"Janie took off."

We stood above the body.

"Janie's gone?"

"This woman is real." I toed at her hip, lightly, tenderly, then knelt beside her. The neck was a mess of black blood, maybe bone, somewhere beneath.

"Sick shit," Max said.

There was a plane overhead, flying low and loud, though we were nowhere near the airport. The plane sounded in trouble. I remember that. I was touching the dead woman's soaked torso with the palm of my left hand, listening to that jet plane, thinking how it might be to fall and fall. I shut my eyes. This woman wasn't cold yet, nor stiff. I felt my pulse against her where she had none.

Max walked to her head, fifteen feet away. "I swear I'm gonna puke again."

"This woman," I said, standing in the easing rain. "This just happened."

"She's young," Max said. "Way too young."

Max sounded like he was crying, or going to. I stood watching. He breathed heavily, his wet shaggy hair draped across his neck and face. He was so skinny then. We both were. He was shivering, but it was not cold. The rain had stopped.

The woman's head looked small beside Max in the middle of the glossed, silent street. Her body was lean. I wondered how that little head could have led this body around, how it could have raced hate and fear and wonderment and love through her, how it could have gotten her into this endless dark pose.

I walked to Max. He didn't see me. He stared at her nearly-shut eyes, and he jumped when I set my hand on his head.

"Fuck Jesus, Kelly!" he said. "Holy fuck Jesus!"

"Easy, Max."

"This is not right. This . . .We gotta call the cops. We gotta find Janie!"

A porch light came on across the street. "Max. Shut it," I whispered loudly. "Shut the fuck up."

We crouched together beside the head, watching for movement inside that cheap little house. The dining room light came on, and a fat, gray-bearded man strolled across the room.

"Why?" Max said, and he began to giggle. "Look at her."

I looked from him, to the woman, back. He was really laughing, and somehow I expected her to join him.

"Ha ha," Max said. "Boo."

Behind the dirty picture window the gray-bearded man paced.

"Quiet," I said. "The fucker's coming out."

"We didn't do this, Kelly." Max poked the woman's forehead. "This is real, but not for us. Who did this to you? Who hurt you like this?"

"More than hurt."

"Who more than hurt you like this?"

The door across the street flung open, and the gray-bearded man burst into the night, the clatter of his screen door echoing. I don't know if he saw us or not. I took off running, as fast as anything, as fast as I saw Janie fly earlier. I felt the drink course through me, and heard Max charging hard behind. I thought of that woman's limp prone body, and her undone, expressionless head. I thought about Janie, about hugging her. I hoped I'd find her, that we both would.

I didn't look back until we made it—somehow—the blocks to Max's grubby one-bedroom bungalow where Janie was sitting smoking on the front steps. She looked so pretty—those freckles and green eyes, that shock-blonde hair glowing in Max's yellow porch light—then she looked scared.

I turned around. Snap. Max had blood on his hands, blood on his face. His eyes were wide and empty. He leaned left, right. The rain had started again.

"I grabbed it," he said. "I ran with her head."

I stepped toward him, and he stepped back. Then Janie was up between us, shivering.

"What?" she said. "What in the?"

"For how long?" I said.

"I don't know."

"She was real?" Janie said.

"Two blocks," Max said. "What was I doing?"

"Very real."

"I flung it into someone's yard." Max looked up, held his hands in front of him, letting rain splash across his palms.

"Jesus." I walked to Janie. The night was a hush, and everything empty. "No one saw you?"

"No one."

"How?" Janie said, as I set my hand on her waist. "My car's back there."

Max rubbed his hands together, and Janie did too. In the distance, sirens.

"No one can know," Max said.

"Right." I motioned Max toward Janie and me. "No one."

"What a poor thing," Janie said.

Max came in close. We were all shaking, trembling. My legs were warm and weak, and we leaned into each other. Janie took Max's hand, and I took hers, and Max led us into the house so we could undress, and shower, so we could lie on his rumpled low bed and sleep through until noon.

ALL HER FAMOUS DEAD

It was the year they were all dying—Mother Teresa and Ginsberg and Jimmy Stewart—and Meredith herself was having a bad go. In March she turned thirty-two, feeling younger and less sure of her place with each week, each hour. She lived alone in an eighth-floor apartment with a south-facing view of Lake Union and Fremont and slivers of downtown Seattle. It was a nice place to watch the world's movements without having to participate, and that's what she'd done a lot of in the months after April when she left her job and started letting Jack pay for her life for a while. Meredith would stand for hours on her little balcony and watch women power-walk past the rusted skeleton mechanics of Gas Works Park, commuters and deliverymen chug ghostly over the Aurora Bridge, kayakers and yachtsmen and sail boaters skim the gray-blue of Lake Union.

At first this turn seemed enjoyable, casually liberating. She saw Jack weekly at bars or restaurants or hotels, and he, as promised, gave her enough money to live out the year jobless, get herself in

137

a better space. Meredith had hated working sixty hours a week, had felt for a long time that she was losing herself in these hours, that somehow she was becoming smaller, less significant. And the freedom was a gift of guilt and seeming obligation from Jack, who had been, and continued to be, Meredith's mother's lover. He was an almost handsome and completely wealthy graying three-time divorcee her mother had met years earlier. Meredith thought her mother probably loved Jack, and that in certain ways maybe now she did, too.

Standing at her balcony that spring Meredith tried to figure a way she could tell her mother, simply to balance the world, but she could never quite assemble the experience in her mind, so she didn't admit anything, not even to herself much of the time. She watched seaplanes and helicopters hum and coast through the rain and began wishing them to fall from the sky, crash into I-5 rush hour, maybe find Lake Union and pierce the water, sink and disappear. Meredith began wishing something like that might fall on her.

On her living room sofa she smoked Parliaments and drank Riesling over ice, eyeing her thin, blonde reflection in the sliding glass door, trying to remember just how she and Jack decided last year to begin. The idea of the emotions and circumstances remained—the lust and opportunity, the slow-boiled anger and pity she held for her mother who'd raised Meredith and her brother by herself, the simple idea of loneliness—but her actions seemed obtuse, part of someone else's life. She wondered, that spring, just how she'd come to live someone else's life, and how this other person had made these decisions. Yet, all she really knew is they had, and that the obvious complications huddled all around her suddenly quiet life.

Then they started dying. And pieces of Meredith whittled away as the papers and magazines and cable news told her all about it.

Allen Ginsberg went first, on April 5th, in the last week she was working. Ginsberg had been her favorite when she was getting her undergrad and still writing poetry. He'd seemed the most genuinely hopeful and wise of the beats, and she still had a worn copy of his collected works, which she thumbed through as one station or another summed up his life with a five-minute retrospective that was mostly just a clumsy synopsis of "Howl." She felt frayed, reading his words and thinking about the brain and hand that bore them now nailed into a box. She began to wonder what was to be left of herself.

At the end of May the musician Jeff Buckley went. He'd been a crush of Meredith's for years. May 29th he drowned in Memphis' Wolf River. He'd either gone for a fateful swim, or intentionally drowned himself—there was speculation. Regardless, he'd washed up at the end of Beale Street. Meredith couldn't think of a worse place for Jeff Buckley to die. She'd been to Memphis once, and Beale Street seemed the beat up, unraveling, worn-down end of what was once a good idea, the wrong place for a beautiful man to end up bloated and identifiable only by his bellybutton ring.

She listened to his slow voice through Seattle's gloomy June, still watching the city teem, still reading Ginsberg, sometimes pretending to sway and slow dance with Jeff Buckley all around her tight living room. Her mother occasionally came across town to ask her when she was getting a new job, and she kept Jack just close enough, but mostly it seemed she was indulging herself with thoughts of Jeff Buckley, feeling like a girl who'd lost her true-love boyfriend.

The empty days were no good, but she got out sometimes and wandered the city. She'd join the produce and craft shoppers at Fremont's Sunday market, or walk over Queen Anne Hill and into downtown where she'd get lost among the quick-stepping businessmen and the crouching panhandlers and the brittle city sounds. Most times she'd end up walking past her old office looking for someone she knew. Meredith never found anyone, though twice she was certain she saw shaggy Jeff Buckley, guitar slung over his wet denim coat, descending Pike Street toward the market. And these wandering days all ended back in her apartment, Meredith opening a bottle or two of wine, painting her toenails green or blue or black, letting the hours dissemble.

Then all these people died, making her feel smaller, and stranger, because she knew them in very certain ways:

Jacques Cousteau, dead on June 25th. Meredith's brother, Carlton, and she used to imitate and quote the great sea explorer at the gem-blue public pool, or up at the cold, green reservoir back in Yakima where they grew up.

Robert Mitchum, July 1st. Her mother once—when Meredith was still in junior high and they were watching a matinee of the original *Cape Fear*—confided that she'd let Mitchum talk her into bed any night of the week. Meredith couldn't imagine it until years later.

Jimmy Stewart, July 2nd. She'd been engaged to a boy in college who charmingly impersonated Jimmy Stewart as part of their foreplay.

Charles Kuralt, July 4th. When she was just a girl her father sold his half of a business, bought an RV, packed up his golf clothes and clubs, then drove away from Meredith and Carlton and their mother saying Charles Kuralt had inspired him to see the entirety of this great country, goodbye.

Gianni Versace, July 15th. She cherished one of his dresses, a pair of his shoes.

Ben Hogan, July 25th. Her father often told them all in the drinking evenings that if he ever learned to hit a 1-iron like Hogan his life would be complete.

William S. Burroughs, August 2nd. Ginsberg's crafty, wife-shooting old bedfellow.

That first week of August, Seattle's weather cleared and warmed. A heat wave pounced and Meredith rented *Mr. Smith Goes to Washington*, *The Night of the Hunter*, old PBS specials of Cousteau, a library edition of Kuralt's best "On the Road" episodes. She bought a copy of the album *That Man, Robert Mitchum, Sings* down at Deluxe Junk in Fremont though she didn't own a record player, and she tried to reread *Naked Lunch*, but ended up simply watching the film.

Then on the last day of August the big one hit. Princess Di. Meredith mostly just wondered what the driver was thinking. She read he'd been drinking, and Meredith figured he'd fallen into believing he and Dodi and Diana and the bodyguard guy were immune, royally blessed. She felt she could understand how easy it would be to confuse that boundary.

September 5th, Mother Teresa. They said she was fast-tracking for sainthood.

Burgess Meredith, September 11th. Her partial namesake. And her brother used to pretend he was the Penguin, from *Batman*, and chase Meredith around their dusty shag-carpeted hallways with a cane and that gravelly squawk. She was surprised Burgess was still alive, figuring since Mick died in *Rocky III*, that the real guy was dead. It made her sad thinking that a lot of people had probably written him off years ago, too.

And on September 17th, when it was 90 degrees and sweaty all over Seattle, and Meredith woke up counting the 136 days she'd been isolated and out of work, and figuring how she was going to finally move on from Jack, and how she was going to finally confess to her mother, and how she was finally going to write a long tough-loving letter to her father who she'd found out was now living in Pensacola, it came on the news that Red Skelton, America's favorite clown, had died. In eighth grade Meredith wrote a report on Red, her first A-plus. She titled it, "If You're Ever Down," after Red's motto which she remembered as something like: "If you're ever down, and I, for even one moment, can make you smile, then my purpose as a clown has been fulfilled." Meredith had always felt that life doesn't get more sadly hopeful than that.

In the warm, still morning Meredith drank coffee thinking about Red Skelton, thinking how she'd maybe include him, and that old

A-plus report, and all the year's famous dead in the letter she was going to write to her father. She figured she'd tell him he could have learned to hit a one-iron as easily in Yakima as goddamned Pensacola. And now stupid Ben Hogan was dead anyhow, so what did it matter. Maybe she'd even tell him about Jack, lie about how she and her mother were sharing him openly. She looked all around her apartment for a decent pen and a piece of stationary, or even typing paper, so she could begin. All she had was a fat felt-tipped marker and junk mail. Later, she thought, tomorrow.

The next morning her mother phoned, said she needed to come over right away. When she knocked loudly, Meredith stood in her robe in the center of her kitchen, feeling the hum of the city pressing through the open balcony door. She felt grounded, and as at peace as she had for weeks, thinking this was good, thinking yes she and her mother should have it out, finally be open adults about Jack, about life. Let the quiet secrets die.

Her mother marched in, sat abruptly on the couch and crossed her thin legs quickly, saying, "Sit down, please." She ran fingers through her dyed auburn hair. "I have some news for you, and I can't stay long."

"Good to see you, mother."

"You're not dressed? I thought you had interviews." She rubbed her hands, pretended to look at her watch. "Would you and your robe please sit?"

"We don't have to be unpleasant about this." Meredith sat beside her, looking directly at her mother, trying to count the lines framing her eyes and mouth. Her mother looked around the apartment, assessing, and Meredith wondered if they could maybe share Jack, and how that would work, exactly.

"I'm afraid this is unpleasant." She turned to face Meredith. "Someone you know has died."

Meredith tilted her head, nearly smiling. "There's been a lot of people."

"Ross Michael, from the old neighborhood, from Yakima, your first boyfriend, or one of them," her mother said.

Ross was a soccer player and a popular guy, Meredith remembered, but kind, always. She'd known him for years, but it had been since high school, since she'd moved to Seattle at eighteen.

"He bought me a charm bracelet."

"I got a call from his mother last night. He was living in Houston. His liver transplant didn't take. His mother and I keep in touch a bit. She lives in Seattle now, not far from here actually."

"Yes. No. I didn't know about Mrs. Michael living here," Meredith said, trying to picture how Ross Michael would look as a grown man—probably a little too short and heavy and tanned. "Liver transplant?"

"I remember that old time. We were all young." Her mother stood, nodding and trembling, holding her arms outstretched. "I needed to come hold my daughter for a minute."

She hadn't hugged her mother in months, and feeling the knots of spine, smelling the fruity shampoo, Meredith pretended to be Jack, wondering if her own body was reminiscent of this, for him. She caressed the small of her mother's back, pressed her tightly shut mouth against her neck.

"Robert Mitchum died this summer, too."

"I know," her mother said, pulling away, looking Meredith up and down. "I read that."

"Red Skelton, too."

"Ross' body's being flown up to Yakima. I'd like you to come with me to the funeral this weekend. It'll be a good drive. We can talk."

Meredith nodded looking away, out the window where a jet traced a contrail across the cloudless sky.

After her mother left, Meredith dressed and went walking down through Fremont and west along the ship canal, four miles through Ballard and all the way to Shilshole Bay where in the hot Indian summer the beach was crowded with families and college boys playing volleyball and old men with metal detectors. She sat among them all on the sand beside a sooty, burned-out log. The air was heavy, sweet. Everyone seemed absolutely alive. She returned three days straight.

That fourth morning her brother phoned from New Hampshire to tell Meredith about a boy named Alex Curry, who they'd grown up living next to.

"Meredith, listen, Mom called this morning," Carlton said. "She wanted me to get a hold of you. Alex was off in Cambodia, or Kuala Lumpur on some sort of feed-the-hungry mission, and he OD'd on some local drug, or drank too much rum, something. The birds were getting to him when they found him on the beach. Anyway, he's dead, too."

She lit a cigarette and sat on her warm balcony. "How would Mom know anything about birds getting to Alex C?" She watched rush hour traffic lurch across the Aurora Bridge. "Jesus, is the whole old neighborhood going to go?"

"It is a tad freaky," he said, and Meredith could hear one new girlfriend or another whisper something at Carlton in the tinny background way out there in New Hampshire.

"A tad, yes."

There were years that Ross and Alex and Meredith were best friends. When Meredith was eight or twelve and summers were always bright blue and 100 degrees, when there were always frogs and salamanders in the gutters and creeks, when there were constantly things to blow up with the firecrackers somebody's dad bought on the reservation. She'd been Alex and Ross' tomgirl.

"Carlton?" she said, twirling her robe tie around her middle finger. "You should come out for Ross' funeral. Fly out today."

"Come on, Meredith," he said. "These people are distant past."

"You could see me, though," she said. "You know Mom would pay for it. They're going to bury him at Terrace Heights. Remember playing hide and seek around those mausoleums?"

"Mom said they're shipping Alex Curry your way, too. His parents still live on the old block."

"You could make it a double-whammy," she said. "Someone else will probably die by the time you fly out anyway."

"Christmas time is when I'll be there, Meredith."

"You're such a good baby brother." She hung up feeling angry, confused. She laughed and rubbed her palms together hard.

Her mother called to ask if Carlton had called. When Meredith told her no she asked if he'd told her about how the birds got to Alex.

"How do you know anything about this?"

"I spoke with his mother at six this morning," she said. "Can you imagine?"

"I didn't know you were still friends with all these people." Meredith reached for her smokes, tried to light one silently.

"What's happening?"

"I asked Carlton to come out," she said. "I have two interviews this afternoon."

Her mother sighed and told Meredith she'd be by tomorrow afternoon to pick her up for Ross' funeral.

"Also, Meredith, please quit smoking."

When she hung up Meredith flipped off the phone and growled, "We should be burying you," but immediately felt trembly for doing it. She walked to the balcony railing, looked down and measured the distance. Tears were coming now and the courtyard eight stories down became a blurry green smear. She chucked her cigarette, and it cartwheeled into the smudge, disappearing in an easy way that she figured could be her fate, too. Fall, fall, go. She gripped the rail hard, shook at the warming iron bars, and cried until she wanted another cigarette. She stepped inside to smoke it, then phoned Jack.

She walked to meet Jack at a café in Fremont. In many ways, Meredith thought, it really was a remarkably beautiful morning. The trees were full and draped fragrantly over the sidewalks; mothers drank big cups of sweet coffee and strollered their children along happily beside businessmen and bike messengers; the light itself, all around her, refracted and bounced off Lake Union and the ship canal and came glowing and shimmering. In those moments, she felt good.

There were two important things Jack said to her that day.

"I didn't know you grew up in Yakima," he said with a mouthful of biscotti.

Meredith had given him the rundown about Ross' funeral, and Alex's foreign death. She'd never told Jack about the old neighborhood, or the horseshoe block where these now-dead boys and she would play kick the can, or shoot air-pistols at Mrs. Wessell's cats. She guessed she couldn't have expected Jack to know, but had somehow figured he did, that he should have. It seemed a betrayal.

She gripped the table edge until her wrist and knuckles ached. "Did you know Allen Ginsberg died in April?"

Jack said, "Why don't we go to your apartment today, after." He nodded toward Meredith's cupped hands, her neck.

They'd only been to her place during the first week of all this. Those mornings he'd told her too many times how cute it was, how charming. And the sight of him walking nude through her own little space had stuck with her. His ease there made her uneasy. She preferred the hotels. Jack himself lived in some eastside McMansion on a street that curved gently back and forth for no apparent reason. He had a maid, and a personal chef. She'd been there just once.

"Jimmy Stewart went down, too," she said. "I wonder if he and

Ginsberg ever met?"

Jack looked at her, tilting his head to the right, she thought, like school portrait photographers always ask you to. He looked serious, and she figured he was thinking about sex, in her apartment, maybe out on her little balcony. He also looked like he definitely felt sorry for her, Meredith thought, like he knew how her insides were knotted and folded over, like he was glad it wasn't him who was losing it. Meredith wanted to grab his silvering hair, shake his handsome musk-scented head until he disappeared. She wanted to ask, "Who are you? How am I still breathing? When will they stop dying?" but she just smiled, took a bite of biscotti. Jack leaned forward, said, "It's such a beautiful day." He took her hands, squeezing gently to say poor girl, poor little girl.

She asked to borrow a pen. He said yes, pulling out a felt-tip just like the one she had at home. When he went off to the bathroom she wrote on one of the café's cloth napkins, "ALL MY FAMOUS DEAD," then listed each of them.

She folded it neatly, wrote, "Read Me" on the top, and walked out into the day.

She walked the half block down to the ship canal and started following the cemented trail east. Joggers and more bike messengers kept chugging by saying "on your left," "on your right." She walked slowly. Tears held somewhere in her chest, waiting to rise. But, she knew, they weren't tears for Jack, not at all. They were tears for Ross and Alex and this stupid death-litany. They were tears for herself.

She let the sun tingle her cheeks and her bare arms, considering going to the interviews she'd set up. But she let that thought pass, figuring she could let Ross and Alex's deaths work into any rescheduling excuse she might want to use to.

Up and down the canal tugs shoved wide rusty barges piled with grain slowly toward the Sound, and high-masted sailboats waited for the Fremont Bridge to draw open so they could have their sunny day on Lake Union. The tears were in her throat now, making it hard to breathe. She stepped off the path, crouched in the tree shadows near the water and began watching the noontime walkers and bikers and joggers round the western bend. These were the people she'd been watching for months. She wondered at their lives, wondered if they ever felt as she did right now—broken and haunted and lonely and mortal. She figured they must, at some point, but that they just weren't showing it right now. Most of them seemed so happy, and together, and she figured that if they happened to look over at her right now they would probably think she was happy and together and satisfied just to be alive on such a beautiful day, too, like them, because that's how most people go through life—putting their beliefs and spirits inside other people.

She shut her eyes, let the tears rinse through, all the way up and out. And as she opened them again Meredith saw Jimmy Stewart and Mitchum and Ginsberg come jogging up the path in a tight little group. Mitchum was smoking, and Ginsberg wore jeans, but they seemed happy and chatty. Then she saw Mother Teresa come pedaling by on a fancy road bicycle, really moving and all geared-up in Lycra, her old flesh pale and loosely wrinkled. Ben Hogan came trudging by, conversing seriously with his heavy black caddy.

Gianni Versace and Princess Diana held their heads low, walking by slowly murmuring.

She was waiting for Alex and Ross to round the bend, too, and maybe come up to her and say hey Meredith, ready for a game of hit-the-bat? Ready to go down to the creek and race paper boats? Who would you rather marry, me or him? Why's your dad always home? Is he really sick, or just lazy and faking like my mom says? All the old questions. But, they didn't show. Her tears cleared and it was just regular people along the path again.

Meredith slipped off her shoes and tiptoed to the cemented wall of the canal, sat and hung her legs over. She wished she had her smokes, but had left them on that table with Jack's napkin note and wasn't going back for them.

Two minutes later a woman came and sat ten feet down from her, dangling her legs over just like Meredith. Meredith smiled and waved, and the woman winked. She wore a little khaki skirt and a blue tank-top, the same thing Meredith had on. Her hair was dyed black and short, like Meredith had worn hers last year when she'd taken up with Jack.

They stared at the choppy canal water for minutes, then the woman took a deep breath and took her skirt and tank off. Beneath she wore a green bikini. Meredith looked herself over and thought maybe she should strip down, too. It was so hot out.

The woman turned, saying, "I'm tired of this swelter. I'm going for a swim."

"Hey," Meredith said, "I almost bought that same suit. Target."

"Target," the woman said, standing, stretching her thin, pale torso. "I suppose it's not deep enough to dive in."

Below them jagged black rocks angled into the canal.

"I didn't know you could swim in this thing," Meredith said.

"What does that matter?"

"I suppose I've been waiting for someone to give me permission." In that moment it seemed just like what she'd been waiting for all summer, the perfect thing, to float the canal with the yachts and the tugs and the occasional crew shell, just backstroke around and feel free for awhile.

The woman did a deep knee bend, then lowered herself gingerly onto the rocks. "You should come."

"I've been crying." Meredith unbuttoned her skirt. "And I don't have a suit on."

"I know." She waved Meredith her way, then made little chicken-wing arms and flapped away.

Meredith smiled looking up into the seamless blue afternoon. In her periphery she saw clown-faced Red Skelton Rollerblade by. She choked out laughter, and in a moment was knee-deep in the cool water trying to balance on a slimy rock.

"Just jump," the woman said, treading water where it was just deep enough.

And she jumped.

Then they were swimming, floating in the shallow margin, and this woman was asking Meredith's name and shouting that hers was Lilly and wasn't this just perfect. Their kicking legs touched here and there. The water was bracing and seemed clean and clear enough to Meredith.

"I've been watching this water go by all summer," Meredith said, treading water beside Lilly, pointing up toward her apartment up on the hill.

"It's been a hell of a hot summer."

Meredith splayed her arms and legs, floating and bobbing with each rolling wake. She looked down at her toes curled up at the end of her pale feet. Beyond them the office buildings and restaurants and taverns and coffee shops of Fremont rose and fell. So did the traffic backed up on both sides of the old steel drawbridge as it began to hinge open. She wondered if Jack was stuck in that traffic, still horny and maybe a little dumbfounded, or maybe just pleased enough that they might be over.

"It's been years since I've . . . swum," Meredith said.

"Swim. Swam. Swum." Lilly coasted up beside Meredith. "Cute underwear. Let's make for the other side."

"Will you take my hand?"

She did, for a moment, and within the gentle lap of that slate-blue water, watching the tall birch trees wave brightly from their posts on either side Meredith felt a generous peace course through her, something she hadn't felt in a long time, a gentle connection. Lilly squeezed tighter at her hand, and it became harder one-armed for Meredith to stay above the divide of water and sky. Kicking, they floated with the current toward the bridge where a cluster of yachts and fishing boats eased toward them.

Over Meredith's shoulder, back near where they'd climbed in, it seemed other people had followed their lead and were swimming now. Five, or eight, or a dozen. Among them she could see Alex and Ross—finally, she thought, they've come—waving both arms above their heads, calling, "Meredith! Meredith!"

"Lilly," she said. She was looking at the sky. "Lilly, I think I see some boys I know. Back where we came from."

"I've always liked boys." She kept hold of Meredith, half-floating on her back.

"Maybe we should go back and say hello."

"Let's get ourselves across first," Lilly said, kicking at the water, yanking at Meredith's arm. "They'll find us if they really want to."

"I used to swim with them," she said, letting herself be tugged awkwardly. "We'd dead-man-float around the reservoir, feel trout or perch pecking at our backs and arms and legs. Sweet boys. They just want to swim again."

"Can you believe that the Penguin died the other day?"

A dark chill ran through Meredith.

Lilly kicked harder, and just beyond each chop in the water Meredith saw the cluster of swimmers splashing around Alex and Ross. She heard her name rise and muddle. Then she and Lilly were in the middle of the canal and the boats seemed all around them, sun glinting off hulls, little shouts telling them to get the hell out of the way.

"Dive," Lilly said, letting go. "We'll meet there." She motioned to the far side where a square of white concrete sloped warmly toward the canal wall.

Meredith was getting colder now and slightly panicked with the commotion. Lilly, in an instant, dove and was gone. Meredith took a lungful of air and plunged, too, scratching and grasping and kicking. Above, a muffled horn bellowed, and she looked up at the golden skin of the water. Oblong shadows slipped and carved. Oddly, she wasn't out of breath at all, and as she kicked and reached and eased deeper she felt a further, profound satisfaction, as if she had solved some great mystery or puzzle, though she wasn't certain just what that mystery or puzzle was—but, specifics didn't matter, it was the feeling itself that mattered. So, Meredith held it. And she shoved deeper, opening her stinging eyes wide, looking for Lilly, or looking for the silty, rocky bottom of the canal, or looking for a big wriggling fish, or Jacques Cousteau, or Jeff Buckley.

But she saw none of that. What she did see was her mother standing at her apartment's front door, knocking away, there to drive Meredith to Ross' funeral. It was a rainy afternoon, cold all over Seattle. The hot summer was a distant memory, and her mother was wearing the fur coat Meredith's father had given her for Christmas one year when Meredith was just a pigtailed little girl.

Meredith sat in her mother's Lexus wearing a simple summer dress and was cold with her mother driving 100 mph, windows fully down, the deep-green piney air whorling all around them as they charged up I-90. Meredith's gut tingled. She lit a cigarette and shivered.

"Here's an object lesson," her mother said, reaching for Meredith's cigarette and taking a long drag, "the birds ate the ears right off Alex C's head. They took part of his nose, too. And of course, his eyes. If you're going to kill yourself by accident, don't do it alone, half-naked on a beach in Indonesia. And Ross. They're going to have an open-casket, but he's not going to look anything at all like the boy who held your hand at the bus stop, nothing like the boy who beat up Roger Neiderman after he called you a dirty, self-involved, cheating ungrateful whore."

"Roger Neiderman said that?"

"Pretty much. Don't be surprised when Ross looks a lot like your father—in those last days before he bought that stupid RV. Do you know how much a new liver costs? Did you know when they replace the bloody thing and sew you back up the scar looks like a Mercedes symbol across your gut?"

Meredith shook her head no, never, and her mother drove on—120, 140—over the pass and into the high, broad land past Cle Elum and Ellensburg where the sky opened up and summer returned, dry and chalky. Then they were in Yakima, walking the Terrace Heights graveyard. At the top of a knoll a man stood murmuring prayers over Ross' naked body, which was not in a coffin, but instead floated in a circle of warm salt water. Her mother waded in. Meredith followed. The prayers floated over the three of them as Meredith traced the three-pronged scar across Ross' sternum feeling electric and sad—for their irretrievable time, for the ways accidents manifest, for the impossibility of what they always thought the world would be—as each moment Ross and Alex and Meredith ever spent together fell as droplets into the pool, onto her mother and herself.

Then they were all around—Red Skelton, Mitchum, Burroughs, poor pecked-at and blind Alex C, Dodi and Di, Kuralt. The hush of their wishing voices rose in the warming, breathless air. Meredith cupped water across her arms and face. The dead all stood in spirals, as the labyrinth, around Meredith and her mother. In her mind, or spirit, Meredith rose above and could see the pattern curling out for blocks and miles, all across the graveyard and the old neighborhood down the block and Yakima itself and the rolling land outside of town. All the acres she knew from her youth were covered with the neatly organized dead. And, trying to listen to the din, she wondered where her place was in this line.

They *all* talked, and it was difficult for Meredith to comprehend just what they were saying. Words were in shambles. Then a "Remember the time!" would rise here, and "I'll tell you what!" would go up there, and a "You're so full of shit!" echoed. She shrugged at her mother, and she winked back, reaching over Ross' bluing thin body to take Meredith's hand just as Lilly had done.

"Round and round and round," she said. "They're trying to tell their stories."

Meredith cocked her head and looked at her mother like Jack had looked at her earlier—confused, pitying. She wished she could tell her mother about Jack, right then and there with Ross floating between them and the warm rain still falling full of history, but Meredith knew she never would be able to tell. It all made her nervous and empty, because she didn't want to feel this, or know this, or be estranged from her mother in any way. She wanted to love her. She wanted to tell her everything she'd ever known. And Meredith did love her mother, she just wasn't sure precisely who her mother was, or how she'd made her, or how someone had made all these people who had come and gone, one by one by one.

"I know, I don't know, I know," Meredith whispered.

The droplets kept falling in opalescent flashes, matting her mother's fur coat, cooling the air around Meredith's head. As the drops fell against her arms and cheeks Meredith saw she and Ross and Alex walking arm in arm and barefoot along the hot asphalt of their old block. She felt the quiver of her sunburned skin. She tasted salt above her lip. It was the day they found a dead German Shepherd in the gully. It was the day her father left. It was the day she saw her mother kiss another man. It was the day a tornado touched down along the Yakima River and carried trout and worn-smooth river stones into the foothills. It was the day she let Ross and Alex feel her up and down as they sat in a full movie theatre downtown. It was the day she moved to the city, hating everything about her old life. It was the day she let Jack take off her dress in her sunny little living room. It was the day they all, each one of these people here, died. It was the day she swam in her underwear through the ship canal.

The rain ebbed and Meredith wondered how long it all could last, when her own history would be spent and returned fully. She stared into the water lapping against Ross. She listened to the shouts and whispers rising.

Meredith shut her eyes as her mother took her arm in a tight grip, lowering the palm into the shock-cold water encircling Ross. And Meredith's breath stopped short as the water wrapped her fingers and wrist, her mother dragging the hand slowly through the pool, hissing, "Swim," into the warm vibrant air. "Swim, my little girl."

MOLLY RINGWALD

Twenty-five years later I'm watching *Pretty In Pink* on Christmas afternoon while my sister sleeps on the suede couch behind me, our parents gone off to church, her daughter in a side room talking to her new American Doll. It's raining hard all over So Cal, and the season seems remotely complete—with me here alone, again, and now the television singing and whispering, disappearing the years as I sit up close eating red M&M's understanding scene by scene that I will never get over Molly Ringwald, or those OMD cassettes, or that fat spray-paint graffiti head shouting at Duckie while he's down and wading in his love for Molly beside STAX, the Smiths record store. I mean, the way she bites her lip, and sneers at James Spader in his white linen sport coat. The way she's smart and precious and a little too thick at the ankles—I love her, too, Duckie, I fucking love her. We're all still in the middle of it, those Psych Furs and New Order songs and Harry Dean Stanton waving surrender, surrender, I gave my life for you—it's what you wanted for breakfast, right?

—

Somehow I got lost in all that Midwest urbania, lost in the dim hopes of big hair and the tiptoe prom dance where the Pogues played the purest future on a three-string mandolin and nothing was easy, but dying was impossible, and I was with you Molly, walking the looming echo of the high school midway and running hallways past the locker bays where Duckie drew blood for you, Molly, because he couldn't imagine his future self without you, and we, all of us, couldn't imagine anything but the joy of the bell ring and the next slow-dance.

Here, the knuckled palm trees sway across the sliding glass, and ocean clouds build towers above the canyons. My sister snores against embroidered silk pillows, and I remember how she wore imitation pearls and checkered Vans and her hair like Molly's that one year—lopsided and coifed—and I wonder if she ever thinks how I hugged her one morning, told her she was cool, which meant that I loved her, wanted a perfect, kind life for her. I didn't yet know this was impossible. I wanted it though, more even than Andrew McCarthy does for Molly, who he takes to that shit party where everyone is shirtless, and drinking scotch despite the fact they're in high school, and Molly's upset because she doesn't drink like a rich kid. Molly frowns that round red mouth. Molly tosses insults and takes a stand. And my sister rolls over, ignoring my niece's back-room whimper, waking only to point at the television and smile above the pile of used ribbons glinting in our dim afternoon. Years fold. And I don't recognize how the one life became the other. Or, what happened to Molly's mother? And did Harry Dean ever get that job? What happened to the way we once loved all this bolo-tie menace and our pony-hair shoes?

And fuck, John Hughes is dead, and he left his cities full of taffeta, left his houses' back doors wide, where someone like me might stumble in to steal his creepers and dance like 1986, live forever on clove cigarettes and mopey antiheroes, and Molly.

But that was only Christmas. It rained all week.

MR. FORMAL

I was working at Mr. Formal, the "civilized good times" tuxedo shop, which was odd and mismatched because truth told I'd never even donned a tuxedo, and was primarily a cynic when it came to formal wear or events where formal wear was required. I was twenty-one, working the front counter full-time—measuring, fitting, running credit cards for prom Romeos and groomsmen all the damned time. I needed a job, but this wasn't what I pictured when I finished high school, did a year at San Jose State, then moved with Dad there to Boise and set up living in the basement of our new house. I had started thinking I could live like an adult, but Mr. F's was like third world, sweatshop bullshit. Yet, as my cohort Bobby always said, "Man's gotta eat, bro." At least I worked at the Broadway store, and not at the mall where horny high school dudes with their wispy mustaches and stringy, mullety hair—endlessly lining up to pay good money for a rented outfit they assumed, along with dinner at Johnny Carino's, would get them laid. Hardly. Carlos, our manager, told me I was good with people—"Stephen, you got smiles for these customers. I like that, shows you know something about civilized good times." That demonstrates what he knew.

Dad and I moved to Boise from San Jose a year earlier when he took a job at the university. Back in San Jose, Mom and Dad split up hard. I watched it all happen up close. They came to hate each other. I guess it wasn't un-typical, but all growing up I was real proud of my folks being together. We were a normal family—going to the zoo, ballgames, Yosemite, the Santa Cruz boardwalk.

My freshman year at State Dad started tutoring after hours and there were whispers around the house, or into the telephone, or when Mom would have Claire and Donna over for margaritas on the patio. She'd been following Dad around, suspecting him of carrying on with some "horny co-ed." Dad taught philosophy at San Jose State, and Mom was like, "Claire you've seen those campus girls—painted-on jeans, dental-floss thongs, cleavage everywhere." Mom's always been an attractive lady—small and blonde and bright-eyed. I can't imagine she had much to worry about. I think she blew up the situation, used it to drive a wedge between she and Dad. "He's started bringing me flowers and taking me to dance lessons to make up for what we never had. He thinks the waltz can save us." Claire and Donna would nod, touch their sweaty, bell-shaped glasses together, and my mother would lean in close: "He's porking one of those little flesh whores. I know it."

I can't say what Dad did or didn't do, I was busy with my own things, my own girls, keeping up grades, keeping my Plymouth running smooth. All I know is things broke down nasty. Mom got overt and started up with some dude from work—Blake or Bernard, some fucked-up name—and threw it in Dad's face. He got mean, telling her: "I'd be happier as a widower," "I hope you have a miserable old age." She got meaner, saying he bored her, repulsed her with that graying beard and concave chest and softening belly, that they should never have reproduced, that he wasn't so smart as he thought he was. I sat in the backyard smoking Camels beneath our dying palm tree and heard it all. Dad got heartbroken, gave notice at his job, applied for this new one, and asked me if I wanted to ride north to Boise with him.

He said: "No more San Jose, Stephen, no fucking more." By that time I was tired of Mom, too. She was aloof, hard-spirited, drinking with her friends most afternoons. She started looking at me like I was a stranger, like she wished I'd just go away. I was different, too, growing into adulthood, making new friends at State, learning important things about the world—like how easy it is for people to fall out of love and turn cynical, how to rub a pretty girl's toes just right, how to rebuild a carburetor, how a mother can resent her hard-working kind-hearted son, how a father can easily be twisted up into resembling another man. Thing is, I didn't want to live in the same town as Mom anymore either, and I told Dad yeah, sure, I'll move to Boise.

And really, I got to like that city, and even relish that Mr. Formal job. Bobby and me made the best of it, got into some good little trouble. You wouldn't think strange, fucked-up shit could go down at a Mr. Formal, but we did our best to make it happen—put cut-out porno pics in tux pockets, Vaseline on zippers, scentless Ben-Gay in the shoes of asshole customers.

Plus, around January we got Franklin working there. Dude. Franklin was very strange—at least to me, right then in my life— probably thirty-five and always talking about Star Trek, or Star Wars, or NASA. The guy read *Omni* magazine, brought a sack lunch to Mr. Formal—V8, string-cheese, slices of slick bologna. Franklin lived with his mother who was supposedly sick with cancer, though Bobby and I thought maybe he had her tied up in the basement, or taxidermied in the attic.

May was supposed to be our busy time—weddings, proms, graduation parties—but it had been s-l-o-w. We were all fallout-shelter-type bored, and Carlos had us doing inventory—counting shirts, bow ties, button studs, all those crappy poly-wool super-creased pants, all those weird satin top hats nobody ever rented. Plus, he had us sorting out damaged items so we could send them out for repair. It was stuffy as hell in the back room and smelled like caustic dry cleaning residue and armpit sweat, plus Franklin was breathing his nasty dead-animal breath all over the place. But, at least it was Friday, and Bobby and I had drinking plans.

"You got a stick a gum?" I asked Bobby.

"Somebody needs to own one." He slanted his eyes toward Franklin who just kept checking items off on the clip boarded list.

"Hey," I said. "Franklin. You holdin'?"

He looked at me like I was a total stranger, like he knew nothing about us being in the room together. Bobby coughed a laugh.

"Holding what, Stephen?" Franklin said.

"Nothin' man," I said, and Franklin went back to his list.

Franklin reminded me of Peter Pfotzer, an old friend of my father's, back when we got on like a good American family. Pfotzer worked with Dad at State when Dad was in his mid-thirties. This Pfotzer was probably Dad's age, but seemed like an old man— stooped, hunched, patchy thinning hair, this yuck onion smell to him. He and Dad drank beer in the backyard after the classes, even though Mom didn't like him, said he creeped her out. I watched her take Dad aside one night, tell him Peter Pfotzer wasn't welcome in her home. He was the only friend I can remember Dad ever having.

"So what's the plans tonight?" Bobby asked.

"Black's havin' that party." Peter Black was a guy we knew from class, a crazy man. Black threw the good parties—DJs, girlies, the whole nine.

"Believe it," Bobby said.

"Retrieve it," I said.

"Men. We are missing two pairs of pants, waist sizes forty-four and forty-six."

"Fat asses likely blew 'em out, Frankie." Bobby said.

"Or dropped a load, gave 'em the toss."

"There's a discrepancy," Franklin said, "we need to answer for."

"You break the news, Frank," Bobby said.

Franklin nodded, checked one more thing off the list, slipped the ballpoint into his breast pocket.

"You *are* the elder authority here," I said. "Tell Carlos the pants situation."

Franklin nodded twice at Bobby, twice at me, and walked quickly out to the lobby.

The house Dad and I rented was in a close, quiet neighborhood—tree-lined streets, quaint bungalows, five minutes from the university, seven from downtown. I didn't even need to drive the Plymouth to Mr. Formal, but I did because where I was from you were nobody if you didn't have wheels.

Everything was so yesteryear there—low crime, and people were all smiles, handshakes. In San Jose we lived in an okay neighborhood, but we hardly knew anybody, and guys would get jacked all the time. That was another thing that upset my mom.

Life was coming together nicely there in Boise. I'd pulled straight A's, met a girl or two, and Dad and I were getting along decently—fixing up our rented house, painting, weeding, planning out a vegetable garden. We'd even driven to a greenhouse one warm, cloudy afternoon, and I'd followed Dad down the long, muggy rows of plants, picking out begonias, Russian sage, California poppies, chrysanthemums. It was the kind of thing I had never imagined doing.

I couldn't picture Dad in that city all by his lonesome. The shit with Mom knocked him into another reality. He was still my Pops, but he was more introverted, more contemplative. Up in Boise he walked stooped, quiet. He patted me on the back a lot. He'd lost weight, toned up, started running again, but drank more. Once in a while we'd share a beer before I went out. He drank imports,

English beer mostly, and he'd talk about the proper way to taste a lager, a stout, an India pale ale. I mostly just liked the buzz, but I listened to him, watched him, thinking that by the time he was my age then, twenty-one, he had *me* to worry about, *me* to feed and hold and change and love like a good father should; and now there I still was, sitting beside him, sharing a drink. Somehow this seemed impossible.

I'd see him on the Boise campus, across the quad, or at the other end of a long, bright hallway, and it would take me a moment to recognize his lanky, head-down gait, his floppy side-parted hair and graying beard, his right hand tucked into that same sport coat pocket. When I'd realize *that's him, that's my father,* I'd think: Man, I hope I don't turn out his way. I hardly knew why this thought came—it made me feel rotten, low, like a son who'd grown up selfish and thankless, though really, I knew I wasn't that way. I loved my father, I just didn't know how those feelings should manifest, or how they would, in me right then, or ever. What I wanted was to understand, to know why I didn't like what I saw as my dad. But I couldn't know. And I started instead to understand that love, family, all the big complex things, would likely always work that way. Frustrating, but inevitable.

Bobby was talking to Carlos beside the Plymouth when I punched the clock and busted out for the weekend. Carlos had hands on hips, and a serious look on his clean brown face. He had mean eyes when he wanted them. Bobby scuffed the pavement with his Adidas. It was a warm night, one of the first of the season—the sky deep blue and rusty yellow, the foothills still green and looking charged in the hard-angled light, thunderheads billowing white above the hills.

"Those pants cost us," Carlos said.

"Especially with all that ass material." I skulked up behind.

"That's beside the point." Carlos swiveled my direction.

"We'll be more careful next time," I said all exaggerated, sing-songy.

"You know anything about joblessness?" Carlos said.

"Relax boss." Bobby threw his hand up. "Pants is pants."

"Ask your parents about joblessness, unemployment, poverty." Carlos was kind of losing it. "Ask them how tough it is to get along in the world when you have no concept of responsibility, when you don't give two shits about accountability."

"Dude," I said. "Chill."

Carlos threw his arms up, too, turned, marched for the front doors.

"See ya bright and early," Bobby said. Carlos kept marching, shaking his head.

"You gotta open?"

"It's fucked," Bobby said. "But that's in the future."

I unlocked the doors and we slid into the Plymouth. Bobby lit a Camel, and we both turned and watched Franklin unlock his bike, squint our direction, pedal toward us.

"Franklin!" I put two fingers in my mouth, whistled. "Hey!"

He rolled to my window. "Gentlemen?"

"Come drink beer with us, Frank."

"Beer?" Franklin squeezed his brake handles. "With the underage citizens?"

"We twenty-one," Bobby said. "Let's go to Buster's. You can buy shots."

I pulled my wallet out, flashed the ID at Franklin. "Just turned this spring," I said. "I'll buy first round, Franklin. Tequila."

Franklin stared at me, or at nothing. "I do like a good tequila."

Bobby catcalled, chanted, "Fran-key, Fran-key."

"Can I bike there?" Franklin held a look—a caged excitement—like he hadn't done a whimsical thing in years and now here was his chance, but he didn't know how to take hold. He looked me in the eye, then away.

"Sure," I said. "Absolutely, Franklin."

"Gentlemen." Franklin squinted like a frail Buddha up into the foothills. "You go on without me."

"Ahh, you're all broke up, Frank," Bobby said. "Mother fuckin' Humpty Dumpty."

"I have Mother waiting at home," Franklin said.

"Mothers know about livin', too," Bobby said. "Ask Stephen."

"Shut your pie hole." I swung an open hand across the back of his head. Bobby ducked, rubbed at his tight-cut hair, gave me the finger. I hated when Bobby talked shit. All he knew about my mother was that Dad once called her a "tramp bitch" in front of him. Dad was just into his cups, that's all.

"You do what you need to, Franklin." I slipped the Plymouth into drive.

"Another time. " Franklin pedaled along next to us. "Next week."

"Tell us another story," Bobby said.

I waved to Franklin and he waved back in a vacant, isolated way that was funny and sad. I watched him diminish in the rearview and wondered how it was to be Franklin, watching Bobby and me roll out through that warm, hopeful air, the plum-colored sky hanging to the east. I thought we were young, living a wide-open life. And I thought Franklin thought that of us, too, and that maybe he was missing his own youth and wishing time didn't move on as it did. He sat on his bike watching, alone in the empty Mr. Formal lot, looking at us, then up at the sky. The loneliest man in the world, I thought—though I didn't really know, and I knew I didn't—as I stomped the pedal and Bobby and I cruised up Broadway.

Buster's was a poor man's Hooter's a mile up Broadway. The waitresses wore short-shorts and half-shirts and most had a nice shape. Bobby and I had been getting familiar—making eyes, tipping like big spenders. That evening Monique was working, and Sara—our favorites.

Standing bar-side, we ordered tall glasses of Bud, Bobby raising his. "To Carlos."

"To Franklin."

"To mother-fuckin' Mr. Formal."

We got through our beers, said hey to Monique and Sara as they walked by holding full trays over their heads, showing the world their gifts. Then, like a golden piece of luck, we had two girls—a brunette and a redhead, both tall and put together—sidling up next to us, giving us smiles and sitting beside Bobby at the bar.

I leaned over. "Ladies."

"Hello," they said.

"This guy," I said, pointing to Bobby, "would like to buy you the drink you want."

"Bobby would," Bobby said, extending his hand.

"Heather," said the brunette, shaking his hand firmly, looking him eye to eye.

"Shasta," said the redhead.

"Stephen," I said, reaching to shake their hands.

Bobby ordered a round of Long Islands and we were off—talking and goofing, getting on wisely, learning all about each other. We moved to a table, and things were going well, it felt like we knew what we were doing. Bobby invited them to Black's party, and they said they'd love to. I gave Bobby a look, and he winked.

I stood waiting at the bar, watching the Friday night NBA game, checking the crowd out as they stitched into each other, everyone smelling like beery cologne and sweet-flower perfume. I turned for the table, and that's when I saw him. Franklin. Sitting solo at the bar, staring into his beer, gripping the glass with two hands. I called his name, but he didn't hear.

"You're not gonna believe this." I sat our drinks on the table. The girls looked at me like, what? Bobby shrugged. And I turned around to march to Franklin.

"Hey." I touched Franklin's shoulder, saw he already had a full new pint.

He jumped, turned. "Stephen."

"What're you doing?"

"I looked for you. This place is crowded."

"Come join the party, bro."

"I checked in on Mother . . ."

I waved and he stood, followed.

"Yo, Frankie, yo," Bobby said, smiling wide. "You made it out of the house."

Franklin nodded as I sat down. "Sit here," I said. "Give the Franklin some room."

Franklin screwed up his face. "I thought I'd experience your youthful subculture."

"I'm down with that." Bobby raised his glass. "Welcome, brother."

I introduced Franklin to Heather, to Shasta, and they grinned, shook his hand, looking at him like, he's a little goofy to be here with us, but they didn't say anything, and it was all good.

"Franklin works with us," I said. "Down the street."

"Right on." Shasta watched Franklin take a mouthful of beer. "Where?"

"In the mines," Bobby said. "Deep down."

"Nah," I said. "We're in formal wear."

"Mr. Formal," Franklin said. "It's a good company—much classier than Friar Tux, or Tuxedo Junction."

The girls raised their pretty eyebrows, drank. The waitress came by and Bobby said one more round, then the party. He ordered Franklin a top-shelf tequila, and Franklin said thank you. My belly was warm, eyes soft, and everything seemed funny as hell— Franklin there beside Bobby and me, beside Shasta with her green eyes and curves.

"So, what," Heather said. "You rent tuxedos?"

"We rip people off," Bobby said. "And the man pays us, like, migrant wages."

"It's a travesty," I said. "Low down."

"It's not so bad, girls," Franklin said. He seemed relaxed, though still somewhat vacant and alone among us, still with that rancid breath. "These two, they live to whine."

The girls flipped their hair. "We work out in mall-land."

"Life's too short to complain," Franklin said.

"Who are you?" I said. "Robert Fulgum?"

"Mr. Hallmark?" Bobby said.

"My name's Franklin, and everything I need to know," I said, mocking, but feeling a little bad about it, "I learned at Mr. Formal."

"Wrong," Bobby said. "In-cor-rect."

The girls laughed and Franklin's eyes narrowed—angry, embarrassed.

"Thanks again for the drink." Franklin stood, slugging the rest of his beer. "Don't be late tomorrow, Bobby." And he started walking.

"Franklin. Don't go, bro." Bobby stood, reached for Franklin, asked him again to stay, said sorry we were just fooling. "Stay, dog. Come party with us, with the girls." Shasta gave Franklin a strong, pretty look, and Bobby turned him, sat him back down.

"Ladies," I said. "Give the man a hug." They did. They leaned in and squeezed Franklin good, reaching up and mussing his dandruffy hair.

—

Black's place was five minutes from Buster's, not far from where Dad and I lived. In San Jose it took at least half an hour to get anywhere. It was a smaller world in Boise. In the parking lot I rounded everyone into the Plymouth. Franklin was kind of wobbly, and the girls were all giggles.

"The girls and me go backseat." Bobby opened the door. "Ladies."

"Can I put my bike in the trunk?" Franklin said.

"Where do you live?"

"Just a ways from here."

"I'll drop you at home," I said, hoping Shasta and Heather might notice my generosity. "You come back for it."

Franklin looked at me squarely, thinking deeply about this. "Okay," he said. "Sure."

We stopped for a case of Natural Ice and two packs of Camels. Franklin offered to pay and we let him. As we drove past Mr. Formal I raised the finger, thrust it out the window, saying, "I got your cummerbund right here, Mr. Fucking Formal!"

"It's a consensus!" Bobby double flipped the place off.

"That's where you guys slave away?" the girls said.

"Gentlemen." Franklin shook his long head. "I can't approve."

I looked at Franklin, shook my own head, as his voice trailed and he looked into his lap. Bobby and the girls cracked a can, passed it around. I drove slow, steady, keeping the music at a medium volume. The sky was orange and turquoise in the rearview. There were new leaves on the street-side trees, and all the air seemed charged.

Traffic picked up with Friday night trucks and hotrods, everybody looking to cruise Main, get a drink, find a woman or a man or a fast new way to live. And there we were among them all.

"Have a drink, Stephen?" Shasta said, leaning to my neck. She smelled so good, like torn-up rose petals.

"Nah," I said. "Gotta survive the drive."

"Arrive alive!" Bobby yelled.

"That's wise," Franklin said.

At Black's house I street parked behind some jacked-up four-by, asked Bobby to hand Franklin and me each a can. The girls sung to the stereo pop song. I turned the volume off, and they kept on, loud and off key, and Bobby joined in. Franklin and me toasted like old-time friends. The beer was barely cold, sour, but felt good in my throat, my belly. I drank deeply, and belched. Franklin did the same.

Black's house was short, squatty, but brightly lit and seemed bigger in the dark. The party was in swing—people dancing and hacky-sacking in the yard, silhouettes shifting through nearly every window. The smell of weed and cloves hung over the street, mingled with the budding trees.

"I haven't been to a party in forever," Franklin said.

"Gotta party sometimes," I said.

"Frankie's gonna get some," Bobby sang. "Tonight, uh-huh."

"I wouldn't know about that," Franklin said. "I do really have to jettison home after this beer."

"Don't sell yourself short," I said. "You're not old unless you act old, unless you think old. That's what my pops always says."

"My metabolism doesn't allow me to imbibe as I once did."

The girls hummed, sipped their beers, singing Bobby's made-up song: "Frankie's gonna get some, get some, get some."

"Let's hit it," Bobby said.

In Black's front yard I told Franklin to come find me when he needed a ride home. Franklin said he lived around the corner, and there was no need for a ride. He shifted one foot to another, definitely on his way to drunk.

"Around the corner?"

"Yes."

"Me, too," I said. "With my Dad. Just two blocks or so, bro." I pointed to my right.

"I'm this way." Franklin pointed the other direction with both hands. "With my mother." He laughed joyfully, and I wondered if I had ever seen him walking, or biking the neighborhood, but just hadn't noticed.

I lightly punched his arm, said, "Mingle with the people." And I headed in.

The house was sweaty air and murmur. Good chaos. I drank keg beer, walked the rooms slapping backs, singing, "Don't stop 'til you get enough," with people I'd never met. I found Bobby on the back patio dance floor, and I shook it with he and Heather. Shasta came to my side, rubbed against my hip, and I felt the heat of her. We were out there four songs before we all got too hot and I decided on some fresh air in the side yard with Shasta.

We sat shoulder to shoulder beneath a wide-trunked tree.

"Smoke?" I lit two Camels, handed her one.

"You ever wear a tuxedo around," she said. "Just for fun?"

"What's fun about a tuxedo?"

"Top hat. Tails."

I put my hand on her thigh. "I'm no magician."

"I'd wear one if I had access," she said. "A white one."

"Only the worst of the cheese wear white."

"But I'm a girl."

"You are that." I kissed her neck. She purred, and I tossed my smoke, moved in with both hands. Shasta and I fondled and tongued each other for a time. Over her shoulder and down her back the party kept on, strangers and friends wandering or stumbling through the yellow haze and thrumming bustle. I felt lucky to be holding Shasta right then—the drink, her full chest against me, put a glow on all this. I pulled away, looked her in the eye, told her I lived real close. She said, that's good, and we got up, made for the Plymouth.

Out front everything was still kicking, too. Through the picture window Bobby swayed beside Heather. Huddles of people sat cross-legged on the lawn, sipping keg beer, passing a spliff. I told Shasta we'd come back for those two, pointing at the window. She took my hand and we walked up the block where Franklin sat on the hood of the Plymouth, knees pulled to his chest, eyes closed, head bowed.

"Jesus," I said.

"Is that that guy?"

"Franklin." We stepped to him. "Franklin, my man."

He looked up, shook his head. "Whoa. What."

I waved. "Yo, it's me buddy."

"Stephen," he said. "Can I get a ride?"

I opened the door for Shasta, got Franklin into the back seat, started it up and rolled.

"I'm not drunk," Franklin said. "No, sir."

"You might be," Shasta said.

"I'm not. I can't be."

"Where you live?" I steered the Plymouth around the block.

"You're going the right way. Just two more blocks," he said, as Shasta ran her fingers up my shirt and across my chest. "That Bobby, damned kept handing me more drinks, more drinks. I don't drink. My mother's sick, she doesn't like me to drink. Stop. Stop!"

I hit the brakes, looked in the rearview at Franklin squinting out the side window. "You live with your Dad?"

"I do."

"Right near here?"

"You got it."

"Park!" Franklin said. "Park it. My dad's long gone. D-E-D."

Before I even stopped Franklin slung open his door, stumbled out, fell to his knees, got up, and lurched for a dark house on the corner. Shasta and I held hands watching Franklin as a slow, warm breeze swayed the branches and rustled the new leaves above us.

He stood at the front door of a brown, wood-shingled place that reminded me of a beach cabin in Seaside, Oregon that Mom, Dad and I vacationed in years ago. The silver-blue light of a television flickered and jumped through the square front window. Franklin opened the door and asked me to come on in, Shasta too, so we could meet his mother.

"Nah," I said. "It's cool."

"Her name's Elise." Franklin looked at the dark ground, reminding me of my father in an odd, tender manner.

I waved for Shasta to follow me in, and she ran up as Franklin fumbled for the light. It snapped on. Franklin flinched, walked through the foyer, the kitchen, into the living room. The house was neat, filled with clean brown and orange '70's furniture. The carpet was a deep shag, pea-green. Across the living room hung a wide painting of Franklin and a woman who had to be his mother. They sat smiling, arm-in-arm beneath a golden-leafed tree. Clouds and little birds filled the blue sky.

I walked to the painting. "This your mom?"

"It took her several months, but I think it was surely worth it."

I eyed the painting, my eyes watering against the sharp, stale-onion smell that was everywhere. I looked to Shasta who'd eased behind me, scrunching her nose, making a face, sticking out her tongue. I looked back at the painting thinking, my mom would never have the patience or love to paint something like that.

"Mom," Franklin said quietly. "Mother?" A figure stirred on the couch in the dim light.

"Frank," came a weak, groggy voice from the pillows and afghans. "Where are you?"

"Right here, Mom." He knelt beside her.

"You smell like a brewery."

"I just had a couple," Franklin said. "Here, stand-up, let's put you in a real bed."

Franklin got his mother to her feet, and next to him in that light, with her long gray-black hair, her thin frame, she looked okay—just a little pale, slightly sickly—and not really a lot older than my own mother. This surprised me, tugged at my chest, made me wonder if I'd ever need to take care of my own sick, dying mom like that. It was something I'd never thought of, and I tried hard to picture it—bringing Mom a cup of water, combing hair out of her eyes, taking her by her thin arm and guiding her off to bed as she told me about her day, as Franklin was doing right then—but I couldn't see it for my life, not at all, and I wondered if that was wrong and selfish, too.

"This is Stephen, Mom," Franklin said. "And his girlfriend. I work with Stephen."

"I know that much," she said. "Give me some credit." She reached out, shook my hand—her fingers cold and hard, so different from Shasta's. "Wonderful to finally meet you. Frank tells me all about you boys at the shop."

"Nice to meet you, too." I nodded, glanced at Shasta who raised her eyebrows, looking skeptical, like she was ready to bolt, like this was all too strange for her. That made me mad at this girl whose last name I would never know. Those people needed us there, in that moment, and I thought she was missing it. "Isn't that right, Shasta?"

"Sure," she said, motioning that we should go.

Franklin eased his mom down the hallway, past wood-framed family photos, through the breach of a dim doorway, and they were gone. Shasta was in the kitchen, opening the fridge, helping herself to a can of soda, and that seemed wrong, too.

"Let's get," I said, tapping her ass as I walked by.

—

In the car I sat quiet, looking out my window, thinking of the long drive from San Jose to Boise. Dad and I took turns driving the U-Haul, the Plymouth pulled behind on a trailer, easing over the Sierras, through Reno, spending the night in Winnemucca. The next day we cruised into the northern Nevada desert and through southern Oregon before we got into Idaho. That U-Haul was like driving slow motion, and Dad and me had plenty of time to talk, listen to music, just stare out at the brown expanse.

Somewhere near the Nevada town of Lovelock I asked him about the Mom situation, but he didn't want to talk about her. Up in Boise, though, we did talk of it a time or two, about how he would never have believed he wasn't just the right man for her.

"Women are slippery," he said more than once, over a bottle of beer, or a cup of gin as we sat at our yellow Formica kitchen table. "You think you're keeping an eye on them, but you never are."

In Winnemucca Dad won $125 nickel-slot jackpot while I was watching a hotel movie, and he brought some of the coins back to the room in a galvanized steel Winner's Casino bucket. Running his fingers through them he said, "A good sign, Son—prosperity lies ahead!" His eyes were red-rimmed, his breath sweet and rotten and boozy. His face held something like happiness.

"Dad, those coins are filthy," I said, though I meant something else.

"Dirty money," he said. "Ha." And he crept toward my bed playing like he would shower me in nickels.

The next day I drove us into Boise, Dad sleeping most of the way. Everything seemed small in a big way, everything new and unknowable—twenty years old, and I'd lived in one house my whole life. It was right, I thought, to have left San Jose, to have come there with my father. I felt like an adult, like I'd made a decision to go, and I'd gone, and now here I was in a place I had never conceived of before. Dad was stoic as we pulled into the driveway of the house he'd rented by phone. I wondered if he thought this was a right thing, leaving like we did, or some kind of permanent failure, a stain on our characters, our persons.

Sitting quietly in the Plymouth beside Shasta I cracked a warm beer, wanting the good buzz to rekindle. I lit a smoke, then one for Shasta. I felt she wanted to ask me what I was thinking, or say she was sorry about rolling her eyes at Franklin and his mother, but she didn't. I knocked down the rest of the beer as we glided the neighborhood streets then back out onto Broadway where traffic was still heavy now at midnight. I put my hand on Shasta's red hair. We listened to the thrum of the stereo and the hush of traffic. I drove Broadway two miles south out to the interstate, turned around, drove back and pulled into the Mr. Formal strip-mall lot.

"This is it," I said, holding up the key as we stood at Mr. Formal's front door. "I know the alarm code. The Man trusts me."

Shasta grinned. "Does he now."

I let us in—happy again, feeling mischievous and sly—deactivating the alarm, walking behind the counter. "Now, it's my understanding that you had an interest in a white tuxedo with tails, a top hat, a cane." It was the first time I'd snuck in after-hours, though Bobby and I had talked about it a dozen times. I was nervous to be in there, but deeply excited, too. I tried to act cool, not to show any of it.

"What was up with that Franklin?"

"Franklin's alright," I said. "He's just a guy I know, a friend."

I took Shasta's hand, led her into the back room where I turned on the lights, got my bearings, then turned them off again. I lay Shasta down beside the cloth laundry bags and boxes of shiny plastic shoes. I unbuttoned her blouse, undid her bra, and she pulled my shirt up over my head. The room was dank and nearly pitch black, and as we rolled around we lost each other for instants.

As I groped and held this girl in the dark, I kept picturing the portrait of Franklin and his mother, the two of them embracing against that tree trunk, amidst all those bright yellows and reds and blues. I thought again about what it must have been like for his mother to paint her own face, and her son's. I sat up, paused in the silence for a moment above Shasta.

"Get back down here, Mr. Formal." She reached to lightly scratch my stomach.

"Yes, my lady." I took her hand, and she pulled me to her.

Soon enough her skirt was off, my pants were off, and we had our sex right there in the Mr. Formal back room. I smelled my breath against her soft skin—orange blossoms and beer—as she hummed sweetly.

When we finished I told Shasta to stay put, don't get dressed. I slipped my pants on, and went to find her a white tuxedo. I rifled through the racks, locating a black one in my size, a white one in what I estimated to be hers. I flipped the backroom lights on, and like a good girl she'd done just as I asked. She lay naked, looking perfect.

"Voila." I uncovered her tux.

She stood, arms crossed over her breasts. "Beautiful," she said. "Can we wear them back to the party?"

"Damn straight."

We did ourselves up, laughing, stopping to give each other the tongue every minute or so, as we slipped into the tuxedos. Hers fit well. Mine did, too. I had never worn one of those things, but it felt good, felt clean and strong, orderly. And I felt important there, wearing that monkey-suit; I felt I was meaningful. I understood maybe why people put those tuxes on in the first place. Shasta pinned her hair up under the top hat. I straightened the back room, then we stopped and took a long look at ourselves in the full-length: Shasta was pure, and I was debonair, and the two of us looked ready to ride off in a horse-drawn carriage. Shasta pointed her cane at me. I snatched it, twirled it, tossed it back to her.

"Double-O-Seven's got nothing on me."

"Take me to a party, James." Shasta stepped up and licked my cheek.

On the way to the party I asked if she wanted to see where Dad and I lived. "It's like three blocks away."

"You live with Franklin, and his mom?"

"Funny girl," I said. I turned left toward our house, thinking it would be damned funny if Dad saw me out there dressed like this. I wondered what he'd say, what he'd think—if he'd even recognize me. The neighborhood was mostly dark, locked up for the night, but as I rounded the corner I saw lights were on at home, and I slowed.

"What's his name?"

"Who?"

"Maybe I've got him for a class."

"Truax. Joseph Truax. Philosophy prof."

"I might have heard of him."

I stopped across the street, and it looked like Dad had left every light on. The curtains were open, showing a bright frame-up of the empty white walls, the thin-legged table of our little dining room, the half-full rickety bookshelf, the stacks of boxes we hadn't ever unpacked. Shasta's cheeks were pink against the tux's white collar—beautiful and ludicrous.

I expected my father to step forward at any moment, to emerge from the back room and look across the street to see his son sitting in his Plymouth dressed in a tuxedo beside some pretty girl in a top hat. I pictured him doing a double-take, squinting, grimacing, giving me a glance that meant *she may look good but watch your step, son.* I pictured him pausing, looking at his toes, then smiling crookedly, giving us the thumbs up. But, the house remained motionless, quiet.

I stepped into the empty street feeling alone and powerful, a mysterious stranger in a vast new world.

"Come on." Shasta ran up beside me, gripped my warm fingers tightly.

We walked hand in hand toward the bright picture window. Our lawn needed watering, but glowed deep-green in the moonlight.

"He's gonna flip," I said, eyeing our thin reflection across the window. We looked like a ghostly wedding cake figurine.

We waited for my father to show himself, and twice I thought I saw his shadow shift in the hallway entrance, but couldn't be certain. Everything remained still, captured. An alley cat darted before us. Shasta flinched. I reached my arm around her, keeping eyes on that lonely, peaceful little home. The wind pressed harder, branch shadows lurching across the lawn. An empty wine glass sat inside on our table, and jazzy horn music played on the hi-fi.

Standing in there, I had never noticed there wasn't one thing hanging on our dining room walls, or even down the hallway. I'm sure we meant to get out old pictures, or frame-up new ones, hang them up where we could sometimes stand and look into the captured faces of people we knew, or ourselves. I was sure we would, eventually, though I can't remember now if we ever did get any pictures hung or not.

The wind died, and I was about to tell Shasta it was time to bolt back to Black's soirée, cut it up some more in our fancy duds. That's when he burst from the hallway—my father—back-stepping and twirling, dancing with an invisible partner. Dancing.

"There," I said. "That's him."

Shasta cupped a hand over her mouth, laughing, pointing. "I've seen him. A friend of mine has him for a class."

"Good god," I said. "Look at him go."

My father did not see us. Fifteen feet away he spun, rose to his toes, smiled coyly. I was surprised as I heard myself laugh, too. "I've never seen him dance."

"This is tremendous." Shasta jumped, pogoed, holding her satin top hat tight.

As Dad reached for the wine glass and brought it to his lips he saw us, and froze—maybe scared? embarrassed? sweetly elated?

"He's had a couple." I quietly waved to my father.

"So have we," Shasta said, and a tingle sped through me.

In a round, muffled tone I heard him through the window: "Stephen! My boy! I'm dancing, dancing!" He foxtrotted toward the window, spun again, tiptoed, twirled, wine glass still in hand.

"Who is this?!" he said, pointing.

"Dad," I yelled, pointing back at him, then at the pretty girl on my arm. "This is Shasta."

"Yes it is!"

"You're a great dancer," Shasta said. "You really are!"

He shuffled slowly, gracefully to the window. "So be it," my father said, leaning his forehead against the glass, rattling the still night air. He looked peaceful, content to be seeing me like that, and I was happier for him than I had been in years, maybe happier than I would ever be again, as he pulled away, rubbed his dark chin-stubble, studying us.

"You're looking pretty good there, Dad!" I kicked at the grass with my cheap, glossy-black shoes, looked up at the rose bushes and neat rows of poppies he and I had planted against our house the week before. I eyeballed the sanded primer around the window frame we would get to painting that next weekend. And what we had been doing together, what we had been assembling, looked pretty good from where I stood right then.

"I planted a Pilgrim Rose. And a Dark Lady." My father smudged his index finger across the glass. "Pick yourself a boutonnière. And a corsage for Shasta, the lady!"

The breeze kicked up, slipping warmly across my face, bringing smells of fresh-mowed grass and Shasta's floral skin. Then the alley cat was back and rubbing against my pant leg, Shasta was tilting her top-hat head to lick my cheek again, and my father was drifting, dancing through the living room, laughing to himself in a way I will never forget.

PROOF

They drove Mangrum's body into town on a flatbed Ford. We'd heard it was coming, that they were delivering proof.

You were at my door, saying they were down at the mall, the body lying suited in a glass encasement. I hadn't seen you in the five days since we'd heard, though I'd been calling, worried. You'd been so low and frightened. This man had taken Heather, your sister, my friend.

"He's here," you said, running pale fingers through your bobbed red hair, the August sky tall behind you. "Put some clothes on. I have to see."

You wore the blue-flowered sundress I bought you for Easter, held your thin arms behind your back. You smelled like soap and sugar.

"What's wrong with my slippers and robe?" I smiled and reached for your waist, but you stepped back and shook your head no. I wanted to comfort you, that was all, be easy and kind as we once were.

"They're bringing him to each city. One by one." You chewed your bottom lip, staring. A crow landed on my front lawn behind you, cocked its neck mechanically, staring.

You touched my forearm, your palm warm and trembling. "Thirty three cities, forty-four taken, including Heather and that girl Claire from South Valley."

"He was a monster, a flawed engine."

Mangrum had taken so many—young and old men, women and girls. Since late winter the previous year, he'd been in our cities taking what we could give him, what he wanted us to give him.

I would read the paper to you in the weeks after Heather disappeared, following his path south, then east, then back north again. It's what you asked from me—to sit on the river bank mornings and tell you the news, and for weeks then there had been news. Those mornings you held my bare ankle and looked across the slow summer river and sometimes cried.

Now he was here, and on my cracked front walk you looked me in the eye to say you were ready, it was time, and I went inside and quietly changed clothes in the warm back corner of my room.

We walked the blocks west and found the crowd gathered around a black truck with a wide silver badge stenciled onto the hood. The glass coffin shimmered, two men with shotguns flanking each end, a dress-uniformed officer addressing so many people we knew—Carlton and Peter who'd been tracking Mangrum themselves, your Aunt Janet and your mother who'd lost such a thing as Heather, just 17, the entire collection of men and women who'd been carrying fear around our city.

We walked the lot, asphalt softening beneath our feet, the air heavy with the last of August, and stood beside a tall woman and her teenage daughter.

The mother touched my shoulder. "I wouldn't believe, if it weren't for this." She pointed over the crowd as the officer stepped to the microphone.

"Did you ever know Heather?" you asked. "Or, any of them?"

"Claire, she was our babysitter," she said, cupping her mouth.

"I was eight that year," the daughter said, hugging her mother.

"Heather was my sister," you said, and began working forward through the crowd.

The officer began, "Now you all might've heard," making a pistol with his hand, "that we took Mangrum out last month, up in Blue Springs, that we found the disappeared, stacked in rows, many rows."

He swept his pistol-hand toward Mangrum, who was angled stiffly our direction—black hair combed slick, pink-painted lips just open, showing slim white teeth, so nearly a common man.

They all applauded.

He continued, "But then, rumors began."

People murmured their versions of hearsay, that Mangrum had kept on, was still alive out there, had been seen in the places we lived.

"But, we HAD him, we sure as hell HAD Mangrum." He reached toward the quieting crowd. "And now you have him, too."

Stairs were moved into place on each side of the flatbed, and a line formed. We were allowed a close look at the thing that had taken so much, and now had been taken himself.

As we moved forward the officer laid out the story of Mangrum's death—the heroics, the gunplay, his final plea of, "Come with me."

Small holes were cut in the head-end of the coffin, and people leaned in, spoke to him, their fists clenched.

Up on the flatbed you knelt and closed your eyes, whispering something I could not hear. I hoped you were simply chanting Heather's name, filling that coffin with her. Long moments later you stood, flattened your dress and flipped Mangrum off.

I stepped up after, ran a finger along the glass-edge waiting for his eyes to snap open, for a smile to curl. I wondered what he loved as a boy, his favorite song, stories he wished to be told. I wondered if he had ever been someone like me, or you, and what had gone wrong.

We descended the stairs, walked into the mall where I bought you slices of pizza and an orange Fanta. The air was frigid and antiseptic. Around us people bought jeans and button-up shirts and jewelry, which you told me seemed impossible.

We weren't young anymore, this much seemed clear even then, and I never truly saw you smile again, which I am so sorry for. By winter we'd leave for good, drift into years and separate lives.

Goddamn the things taken.

But, that night after you spoke to Mangrum you lay tight beside me letting me hold your waist and hip, and at dawn we walked to the freeway overpass hand-in-hand to watch the flatbed steer into the near lane, blue tarps billowing over Mangrum, diesel rev rising as they drove him west into the still-dim horizon.

FALSE HISTORY

Jeffery is swimming with Allison, his daughter, watching the white sun fold upon itself a thousand times across tiny blue waves, within the lovely timbre of Allison's asking—"Throw me, Dad. Dunk me!" She is a thin, freckled girl with one missing front tooth. Smiling. It is a hot afternoon, easily one hundred degrees, and the splashed water dries quickly on the beige cement ovalling the pool. Caroline, Jeffery's wife again, sits in umbrella shade, smoking a menthol cigarette, watching the two of them laugh and lunge and tumble through the shallow end.

Allison is six. Jeffery and Caroline are twenty-eight. They are all in Jackpot, Nevada in the last week of July. A family together, on the road back from Vegas, where yesterday afternoon Caroline and Jeffery looked into each others eyes and murmured vows again after three years of divorce. The Everlasting Truth Chapel. It seemed a trapped white place to Jeffery, and he wonders if he may soon forget the Reverend Clyde Cunningham's throaty commands, his cigarette breath, the tinny recorded organ chords. He wonders if he will forget Caroline standing in her strappy yellow dress, looking up at him with eyes that said thank you, again, this will be right, we were married three and divorced three, that makes this all an even thing, you are a good man. Jeffery wonders. He knows he will never lose this part of how it felt: Allison balancing on one foot, then the other, beside him in her orange-flowered dress, her white-gloved fingers squeezing his hand hard, so pleased.

The pool water is tepid, but clean and cool enough to be refreshing beneath the charge of this blue sky. He can smell the desert through the chlorine as he looks over his shoulder toward the spotty yellow hills cresting and shifting in the heat. Jeffery takes a full breath, falls backwards into the wrap of water, and he hears Allison squealing as he lets himself sink and lay flat on the pool's gritty concrete bottom. He hears the echoed words, "Daddy's foolin'! Fake drowning again." The warbling rumble of Allison's kicking and slapping as the water presses into him. He opens his eyes, watches her silhouette lurch and bounce within the bright ripples.

Caroline's voice slips soft and full: "Jeffery!" she says. "Jesus."

"He's such a faker," Allison says, and Jeffery bubbles the held air from his mouth. He sees Caroline standing at the lip of the pool, one hand on her hip, the other holding a beer can.

"Hey, Houdini," Caroline says, and he waves. "Come join the living."

His chest is tight, his head feels like it's coming apart, and he thinks, I smoke too damned much. He pushes himself up and grabs Allison around the waist. She is so thin, so light, as he throws her, arcs her into the center of the pool.

"Hot damn," Allison says as she rises to the surface.

"Young lady," Caroline says. "Language."

"He's alive," Jeffery says. "Alive!" He flexes his biceps, growls.

"Apparently so," Caroline says, and saunters back to the chaise lounge, shaking her head, her sandals clip-clopping against her heals, against the hot cement. She has hips now, Jeffery thinks, more than she used to, and meat on her arms. He watches her shift and settle, light another cigarette. Jeffery has known her for so many years, since they were fourteen, sophomores at Boise High, and he has always liked the shape of her, the sway and rhythm of her walk, the exaggerated gestures of her anger, the contours of her laughter. He has liked her thin, and now is drawn to her heavier shape. It can't matter what she will ever become, he thinks, and he is surprised at this admission.

"Don't pay her no nevermind," he whispers to Allison as they hold onto the pool's edge and eyeball Caroline. Allison plugs her nose and thrusts herself beneath the surface. He pinches his own nose, and follows.

They are staying at the Horseshu Hotel and Casino in a pool-view room, #309, the Antelope Wing. Jackpot seems the funniest of funny little nowhere places to Jeffery. A wide spot along Highway 93 at the Idaho border. Five casinos, and clusters of trailer homes. He has been here a dozen times since he turned twenty-one, to gamble, to drink and feel like he was away from things known. Jackpot seems to Jeffery perfect and unlikely all at once, and as he crouches within this water, feeling Allison tug at his shorts, it seems exactly appropriate, unquestionable for this moment in his life. All around them this desert valley lolls and dips in patchy shades of brown encircling the barren golf course, the tiny airport, the trailer homes and short apartment buildings. The wind pitches thin and warm. Jets trace contrails, marking X's in the seamless blue.

The three of them rolled in this morning, sitting hunched and tired in the Pontiac. They had driven up Highway 93 through the night, the four windows fully down, pulling the dense night air around them, the guiding sliver-moon barely lighting the straightaways. Caroline said they couldn't afford a true vacation, that they had to get back to the apartment, back to work, but he felt they had to have something to top-off this remarriage in Vegas, this sudden togetherness. And the poolside cocktails, the swimming with Allison, the tingle and burn of sunshine on his chest, his face, Jeffery believes this all is something, even if it is in Jackpot.

He slips out of the pool, leaving Allison behind. "A damned fish," he says, sitting in the pillowed chair beside Caroline. "My girl's got gills."

"I've been taking her to lessons."

"She's amphibious."

Caroline rolls her eyes. "These people here," she says, scrunching up her nose, eyeballing the scene. Dotted around the pool are four older couples and a cluster of heavy-set women reading books with bent paper covers, drinking orange or red drinks. A younger couple—the man with a short beard and a silver necklace, the bony woman in a white string bikini—sit dangling their shins in the deep end. It's a small pool. Allison is the only child here.

"It's not Mandalay Bay," Jeffery says.

"Clearly."

"You got a beer for me?"

"Maybe we should've put it on the card."

"That's a load," he says. Caroline hands him a beer from the six-pack cooler. The can is cold across his palm as he snaps it open and takes a full swallow. "We've tried that before."

Caroline closes her eyes, then smiles, then opens her eyes again. "How'd you stay so skinny?" She pokes at Jeffery's rib cage. She touches at his wet hair. "We should get you a cut this week."

"I'm just built skinny."

"Look at this," she says, turning her hip out, grabbing at her left butt-cheek.

"Grade-A," Jeffery says. "A fine piece."

Caroline snorts, takes a drink of her beer, and she leans to kiss him. He leans into her as he hears Allison's wet feet padding toward them.

"Ooch. Eeech," Allison says. "Hot as hades."

Allison sits on Jeffery's lap, and he asks Caroline to hand him another beer.

"Drinking a lot today. "

"It's an occasion," he says, and holds the can to Allison's neck.

"Ahhh," she says.

"An occasion," Caroline says, and they touch their beers together. "How does a person just get bigger?" She grabs at the flesh of her thigh.

"Cell regeneration?" Jeffery says. "Genetic history?"

"What's to stop you from just growing and regenerating," Caroline says. "Just widening out all over the place. What's to stop me from becoming ten me's?"

"We could do with ten you's," Jeffery says. "Isn't that right?" He nods to Allison. She nods back, and looks toward the couple at the pool's edge.

"So that's how you feel now?" Caroline says.

"Just about."

"Well, I'll ask you again when I become ten me's."

Allison turns to Caroline. "Gravity'll stop you," she says, "from becoming ten you's." Across the pool two of the older men stand shirtless above the deep-end. They look to each other, gather themselves and leap, cannonballing into the bright water.

"That's probably right," Jeffery says. "But it doesn't matter if it isn't."

"Gravity?" Caroline says.

"It keeps us small," Allison says.

In the room Jeffery shakes his head and hops on one foot, trying to jar water from his ear.

"What're you playing tonight?" Caroline asks.

"Slots," Allison says. "Keno."

"No," he says, still hopping, watching Allison stand beside the surging colors of a television game-show. "Damned ear's plugged up."

"Craps," Allison says, and she jumps up and down beside

Jeffery, sticking her finger in her ear.

"The Horseshu has two-dollar twenty-one," Caroline says.

"That's where you'll find me," he says. "To start with."

"Maybe roulette," she says slowly, walking toward the window. "Not too heavy, though. Rent's up in a week."

"I wanna play Wheel of Fortune," Allison says. "Or Jeopardy."

"You can watch cable television," Caroline says. "How's that?"

"We'll play keno at dinner." Jeffery quits jumping, and the water is still in his ear. What if it stays there forever? Could he ever get used to this tedious sensation, the muffled tension of sound waves pressing through this water?

"You know what I heard once?" he says, pulling Allison to his lap as he sits on the polyester bed-slip. "I heard about a woman who had the hiccups for twenty-three years. Couldn't lose 'em for anything."

"Wow," Allison says, faking a hiccup. "That's like magic."

"They gave her brain damage."

"Because she held her breath all the time? Because she drank water all the time?"

"Don't believe any of it," Caroline says. "You're dad has a million. Eventually, you'll hear all you need to hear."

"It was because she got so mad about the hiccups that she kept banging her head against walls," Jeffrey says.

"Twenty-three years?" Allison says. "Holy moly!"

"It's true," Jeffrey says. "She lived in Baltimore."

NAKED ME

—

Dinner is the Cactus Pete's International Buffet across the street from the Horseshu. The waiting line snakes into the casino, and the three of them find their place to stand. Caroline holds Allison's hand. Jeffery looks around, scopes the action. Orange and yellow lights flare, riding a current of loud hollow noise—bells, horns, whistles—into the dim casino air. Jeffrey stands utterly still, feels the flashes of sound pulse through him. It is early, and not busy yet. The slot machines stand polished and orderly, lined up with one or two older women amongst them, feeding bills in, pushing buttons. The weighty ring of spilling coins sporadically rises, spreads through the casino.

"Looks like people are eating," Caroline says. "Not gambling."

"Will you play the Monopoly slot for me?" Allison says.

"Maybe later," Jeffery says. "Which machine is the lucky one?"

"That one!" Allison says, pointing. Caroline pulls her close as Jeffery looks across the casino floor at the uniformed dealers standing, hands behind their backs, at empty tables. He wonders: How did they get here? Do they like living in Jackpot, Nevada? Has the action, the movement, become ordinary, or does it wind them up as it does me? Might they wish they had never come?

He looks back to Caroline and Allison amidst a cascade of glitter-light. He wonders, as he has, what it might be like to pick himself up, leave his job and friends and life, and come work and live as a new, anonymous man in a small foreign place like this. He watches a young, blonde dealer scratch her nose with a long blue-painted fingernail, and his chest feels hollow and sad. Jeffrey squints, stares,

202

tries to read the woman's nametag—Heidi? Helga? Helen?—as he feels his daughter tug at his pant leg. Caroline is wiping Allison's face with a tissue, Allison is making a face, and Jeffery thinks he is pleased enough to have returned to Caroline, that they have returned to each other.

"You gonna go Mexican, or Italian?" Jeffery says. "Or maybe Chinese?"

"Italian," Caroline says.

"I'm going global," Allison says as sirens and bells rise from a hidden row of slot machines. They can hear a woman yelling: "Ten Grand! Ten Grand!" Jeffrey's heart speeds, his fingers tremble and sweat, and they all raise their eyebrows, shrug, smile at each other.

After dinner they walk Allison to the room, dress her in the nightgown with the tiger and elephant print. Allison protests quietly, but she is tired. Jeffery turns on the television, and the three of them sit and watch a black-and-white noir film where a man staggers, holds his heart, and dies bloodlessly. Jeffery opens a beer, hands one to Caroline. She nods to him, and lights a menthol. Allison falls asleep quickly. Jeffery looks from the television to Allison. She is breathing so evenly, her thin ribs wrapping her heart, her tired head something like his. Jeffery is certain he will never sleep like this again. He looks to Caroline, who is watching the flickering action of the television, and he is worried for them, for all of this, and he isn't sure why.

"You ready?" she asks, standing, snubbing her cigarette in the glass ashtray she holds.

"That water's finally outta my ear." Jeffery nods, walks to Allison, kisses her soft, freckled hand and cheek as Caroline stands above them.

"That's a relief."

"She's wiped," Jeffrey says, feeling his quick, rough pulse beat against Allison's.

"She's gone to this world," Caroline says, tapping the top of Jeffrey's head. "Let's get it going."

They make their way to the Horseshu's casino where they find seats at the two-dollar blackjack table. The casino is small and low, paneled in grainy wood, a different look than Cactus Pete's. The room seems crowded at first to Jeffery, full of action and possibilities as shouts and laughter bursts from dim corners, from men huddled over the craps pit, or women playing Spanish 21. But, as he sits and begins playing he realizes that it is temporary—the jumping lights, the thrumming music seeping from the bar, the mingling slot-machine bells. A chaotic artifice. A sweet falsity.

They play for two hours, Caroline winning, Jeffery holding near even. The waitress brings them Cape Cods, and they tip her fifty-cent pieces.

"Hit me in the right place," Caroline says, and she squeals when the dealer lays a five of diamonds on top of her two eights. Jeffery slips his cards under his red five-dollar chip. The dealer hits on fourteen, slapping a jack of clubs onto the table, busting. Jeffery nods his head when the dealer sets a red chip in front of him.

Jeffery stacks his chips—forty-five dollars—stands, stretches, then drops the chips into his pocket. He is so tired, but holds no want for sleep. He watches Caroline play and win three hands. He taps her shoulder. "Think I'm going." He nods toward the door. "Check the Cactus action."

"Alright," Caroline says. "I can't leave this seat."

"Keep it hot," he says, bending to kiss her.

Across the street the casino is full and seems brighter to Jeffery than before. Shouts rise from the craps pit, and a dull musical weave fills the yellow air. An R&B band is playing above a half-moon bar, the bartenders pouring drinks as the lead singer shuffle-steps just over their heads. Jeffery sits at this bar, feeds a twenty into the video poker machine, orders a Wild Turkey rocks. He drinks it fast, and feels new blood course through his neck, his face. He raises his hand, orders another. Jeffery lights a cigarette, spins in his seat, and looks out across this room—so much movement here, he feels it seeping into him, winding him up, but he feels he is not a part of it. He watches a gray-haired woman dance with the band's lead singer as he traverses the crowd with his cordless microphone.

"My little girl would like to boogie like that," he says toward the man sitting beside him. "She dances like a Solid Gold girl. You remember Solid Gold?" And he smiles thinking of Allison sleeping, clutching a peace that he craves. "You wonder how anybody sleeps after being in here."

The man beside him points at his ear, then at the band. Jeffery nods. He gulps his drink, stands. "I'm a newlywed," he says. The man beside him shrugs. "Dually wed." Jeffery presses the cashout button and twenty-dollars in quarters rains loudly from the machine. Jeffery scoops them into a plastic bucket, and he begins walking the casino floor, watching the men playing table games, watching the cocktail girls balance trays of empty and full drinks. He cradles his bucket of quarters as he finishes his cigarette, and walks out the front door.

Jeffery sidles across the street, feeling a little wobbly. He thinks he might want another drink, but he's not sure. "Maybe I should go find that woman," he mumbles to himself. But, he decides not to, decides to let her have her own fun. He'll have plenty of time to see her now. Jeffery instead walks into their hotel and climbs the stairs, then hops the short poolside fence to go sit beside the water.

He is the only one there. It is dark all around, but for two pool lights. The water is a gem. He sits in the same chair he sat in hours ago, lights another cigarette, begins thinking of how the time was without Caroline. There was only one other woman, and it was something he could not enjoy. Danielle, a woman he met on the street, buying a sandwich on her lunch break. She was thin and dark. He took her to the bar a few times, and she wanted to hold his hand as they drank. They shot pool and threw darts and she took him to her house where they undressed each other and she stood naked over him as he lay on the blue sheets of her bed. Her shape further shadowed the heavy air between them. Danielle whispered words he never heard into the lavender and sweet peach smells of her room, smells that for Jeffery held Caroline, held Allison, dissembling his movements, his desires. After two weeks Jeffery couldn't see her again, and told her straight. Danielle said she understood, though it was clear to Jeffery she didn't.

Beside the pool Jeffery leans into the chair's soft fabric. The stars are a smeared contrast, shifting in his half-drunk vision. He wonders how maybe they've ruined things for each other, Caroline and he, taken the pleasure from what should be pleasurable. But, he supposes, there is a balance to all this. He reaches into his quarter bucket, lifts a coin and tosses it into the green-blue water. It plunks hollowly and flutters to the pool's floor. He throws three more coins, wondering if this is a wishing well, realizing he has forgotten to wish for anything.

Across the way a room light pulses on. He sees a figure open the blinds and the window, then turn away. Jeffery recognizes the woman, he thinks, from somewhere. She returns to the window with a lit cigarette, and his chest tightens realizing it is Caroline, of course. Jeffery catcalls her, whistles. Caroline waves back silently with her cigarette hand, the cherry tracing shapes. He stands up, walks to the pool's lip, feigns falling in, tiptoes along, play-acting like he's on a tightrope. Clutching the quarter-bucket in one hand, there is no sound but the shifting coins, and he feels strangely like a man inside a television with the sound turned way down. Jeffery stares at his shoes, balancing the edge—mint-blue water, still-warm pavement—and as he hears Allison laugh he looks up smiling to see the two of them, these women he will always know, arm in arm, pointing his direction.

ACKNOWLEDGMENTS

So many thanks go to Dock Street Press for their righteous support and enthusiasm in getting this book out into the world. Cheers forever to the writers and kindred souls of The Gamekeeper Salon—Carrie Seymour, Matt Moorman, Mathew Haynes, and Lorie Chastaine. To the talented and inspirational students of The Writers Write Workshop and Boise State's creative writing program. To Mitch Wieland, Robert Olmstead, and Tony Doerr who helped me build the foundation this book was built on. To my loving family and friends.

CHRISTIAN WINN was born in Eugene, Oregon, and grew up in Palo Alto, California and the Seattle area. He now lives in Boise, Idaho where he writes and teaches in the Creative Writing Department at Boise State University. He is the founder of the Writers Write fiction workshop series, which has been in operation since the summer of 2003. He is a graduate of Seattle Pacific University, and the Boise State University MFA program.